CAROLINA HOMECOMING

ALSO BY HEATHER BLANTON

Grace Be a Lady

Hell-Bent on Blessings

A Scout for Skylar

Locket Full of Love

Romance in the Rockies Series

A Lady in Defiance

Hearts In Defiance

A Promise In Defiance

Daughter of Defiance

A Destiny in Defiance

Hope in Defiance

A Reckoning in Defiance

In Time For Christmas: A Novella

CAROLINA HOMECOMING

HEATHER BLANTON

And a big thank you to Lisa Coffield and Trudy Cordle for their edits!

FOREWORD

Dear Reader,

Being in a *Christian bubble*, it's easy to forget that not everyone knows their Bible. I was participating in a Facebook party to promote Carolina Homecoming when a reader told me she wasn't familiar with the story of Ruth, Naomi, and Boaz.

If you have never read this family's inspiring story of love, friendship, and loyalty, I encourage you to check out the Book of Ruth. It is sandwiched between Judges and First Samuel in the Old Testament of the Bible.

To summarize, Naomi was an Israelite who moved with her husband and two sons to a foreign land during a famine in Israel. The boys grew up and married Moabite women, pagans, but then the young men and their father were killed.

Heartbroken and downright disgusted with God, Naomi threw up her hands in despair and declared she was going back to her own home place in Bethlehem. She suggested her daughters-in-law go back to their people.

However, one of them, Ruth, refused to leave Naomi and accompanied her back to Israel.

Times were tight and finances slim for the two ladies. Naomi told Ruth to go glean in the fields to put some bread on the table. It turned out, the field she picked belonged to a man named Boaz, a distant cousin of Naomi's. He saw Ruth working like a dog and asked about her. Well, word travels fast in a small town. Everybody knew she was Naomi's daughter-in-law and that she'd been widowed but had refused to leave her mother-in-law's side. Boaz was impressed with the young woman's loyalty and ordered his servants to let her glean undisturbed as well as throw a little extra wheat her way.

When Naomi heard about her cousin's generosity, she must have gotten that certain matchmaking twinkle in her eye. Being that Boaz was kin, he was entitled to claim her homestead, the girls along with it, and provide for them.

Naomi instructed Ruth to go to the threshing floor after everyone was asleep, find Boaz, and curl up at his feet. This was a sort of marriage proposal, and Boaz was all in. Apparently, he and Ruth had spent the Barley harvest falling in love. Yet, he seemed surprised by her offer and mentioned how he appreciated her ignoring younger men to choose him. This suggests to me that he was sensitive about his age. Perhaps he saw himself as too old for Ruth? Fortunately, she corrected him of this erroneous thinking.

By law, however, the couple still had a hurdle. There was another man in town closer on the family tree than Boaz, and therefore, with more legal standing to make a claim. First in line or not, this fella didn't feel like taking on a wife and a mother-in-law, and he stepped aside, clearing the way for our hero and heroine to marry.

Praise God, they did! They continued a bloodline that

led to King David and then right on down to the very King of Kings himself—the Lord Jesus Christ!

Now that's a couple that was meant to be together. I urge you to read this beautiful story in the Bible. By the way, Noemie— No-em-y— is the French spelling of Naomi.

Anyway, I hope you enjoy my fanciful version. I am from the mountains of Western North Carolina. I love the people, the culture, the landscape. Come, walk with me through the Blue Ridge Mountains and the foothills of South Carolina...

CAROLINA HOMECOMING

CHAPTER ONE

RUTH WONDERED HOW SHE WOULD FACE ANOTHER DAY, strangled as she was by grief and guilt.

The spring breeze through her window chilled the tears in her eyes and she dabbed at them angrily. "This is no time to be a whimpering sot, girl," she chided, her Irish backbone attempting to buoy her spirits. "Oh, James," she whispered and sat down again on her bed. "Why did you have to go off and die?"

From the parlor, she heard Noemie sniffle, and Ruth winced at the reminder. Her mother-in-law was suffering, too. The war had taken James and left two women struggling with the loss. For Ruth, her husband's death stung, yes, but it wasn't debilitating. He had been a good man, a good provider, even a good friend, but not much of a husband. For Noemie, though, he was the son she'd borne from her own womb. Ruth couldn't imagine the woman's pain and she ached for her.

Closing her eyes, she whispered a silent prayer for more understanding and compassion and rose to take on the day. Her swishing, black, hoop skirt announced her entrance as she stepped into the parlor. Noemie didn't react. She was standing at the window, a handkerchief pressed to her mouth. Her face, still fetching for a woman of fifty, was a mask of pain. Furrowed brow, clenched jaw, and red-rimmed eyes.

Surprisingly, she hadn't dressed yet. Her hair was not twisted up over her head in the crown of braids she preferred. Instead, thick blonde and gray strands cascaded down her back in an unbrushed torrent. And she was still in her nightgown and robe, not her black dress of mourning with its voluminous hoop, like Ruth's. She looked older this morning, her years amplified by the soul-tearing grief.

From outside came the well-timed, almost melodic steps of two hundred feet marching down the brick avenue. The sound was somber, like a funeral dirge.

More good boys headed off to this vile war. "Noemie, are you all right?" A foolish question, but it seemed the only one to ask.

The woman blinked, but still took several seconds to answer. "I've come to a decision." She turned faded green eyes to Ruth. "I'm done with Maryland. I'm going home."

"Home? I don't understand. I thought Maryland was your home. I mean, I understand you're not from here, but ye've lived here—"

"Ten years. Almost ten years here with Jeremiah. He was my second husband. A good man. I loved him, but Maryland was his home place. I've got more years and more roots back in South Carolina." She paused briefly, as if reliving a flood of memories from those days. "James's daddy, Luke, and I were both born in Oconee County. We did a lot of living there before he widowed me." She turned away from the window to face Ruth. "And then Jeremiah went and died on me. I only stayed here after his passing because I hoped you and James might start a family. And then he left you to go fight in this blasted war." She raised her chin and straightened her shoulders. "I've held on to the place in Oconee County. It's time for me to go home."

Ruth reeled from the news. She opened her mouth to speak, but only squeaks came out. The babbling seemed to spark more alertness in Noemie. She smiled tenderly at Ruth. "I want you to go on back to Ireland. Go back to your home. Bid this horrible war and its losses good bye."

"I don't want to." Ruth crossed the room and took the older woman's hands. "Please, don't send me away, Noemie. I love ye like me own mother. I've no one else left in County Cork that matters to me."

"And I love you like a daughter, but I want what's best for you."

"And that would be staying here."

Noemie pulled a hand free and motioned to the room. "Then you can stay here in this house, if you're of a mind to." She patted her fingers reassuringly. "You're still young and pretty. I'll see you're taken care of till you marry again."

"No, I want to go with ye. Ye need me."

Noemie's brow shot up. "I need you?"

"Aye, to take care of ye."

"I'm fifty, girl, not eighty, and 'bout as fit as you are."

"But I can't let ye be alone."

Noemie took a step back, shook her head. "In fifteen months, I've lost my husband and my son. I reckon God's turned His hand against me, Ruth. Best you not be around me."

"Ye wouldn't want me to break a promise to your son, would ye?"

Noemie's emerald eyes widened and glittered with shock. "What promise?"

"I promised him I'd take care of ye. I gave him my word."

"He had no right to ask you for such a vow."

"I made it. And I made it gladly. I'll not leave ye, Noemie. Where ye go, I will go. Your people will be my people..."

"And my God, your God." Noemie smiled, but there seemed to be little joy behind it. "All right. Then let us put our hand to the plow and not look back."

———

RUTH HAD no idea what to expect on the journey back to Noemie's birthplace, other than she suspected two women traveling alone amid a war might be a little brave and a bit foolish. As they crossed from Virginia into North Carolina, they read a newspaper reporting on the battle of New Bern on the coast. The number of casualties, though small, brought tears to both women's eyes.

Passing into South Carolina near Charlotte, they again heard of fierce battles, but now up in Virginia, some place called Shenandoah. As Ruth lifted the lid on their Dutch oven to check the stew, Noemie pulled her writing satchel from the wagon and sat down near the fire. "How's it looking?"

It was hard to see in their campsite a few yards off the road. The flickering flames of the small cook fire gave off only meager light, and Ruth couldn't rightly tell much on visual inspection of the stew. It smelled wonderful, however. She swung her braid out of the way and dipped a spoon into the broth. Blowing off the steam, she tasted it.

The bacon had flavored the cabbage perfectly. "In my humble opinion, I think it's the best I've ever cooked."

They settled down to eat and Ruth offered a quick grace. "Thank You, Lord, for bringing us safe thus far, for loving us, for keeping our spirits up though our hearts are broken, and thank You for this meal. In Jesus's name we pray."

Ruth took a sip but noticed Noemie practically glared at the soup. "I think He's contrary and not so mindful of us. I've had enough grief at His hand, and I don't want any more."

Ruth took a deep breath. Noemie's anger with God, though understandable, was heartbreaking. "God didn't kill James. The war did. Man's penchant for fury and violence took him. God is good and He loves us."

"Then why didn't He protect James?"

Ruth had asked herself that question a thousand times. She could only give the answer that seemed right to her. "James rushed up a hill into a hundred Confederate guns." She could see her husband doing so, his brashness was one of the things she'd loved about him early on.

She swallowed the knot in her throat. The memory of him, the way they had started out—hopeful and lost in each other—always saddened her. Love seemed an easy thing for some to take for granted. "Men die in war," she told Noemie, almost absently. "'Tis the way of it. 'Twas his time."

Noemie merely grunted and attended to her soup. Ruth said no more. Her mother-in-law needed time to heal. She only prayed the anger would be a wound that would fade and leave no trace.

The two women ate in silence for a few minutes, but questions raced through Ruth's mind, especially one. She asked it every night. Now she would ask again. "Where are we?"

"Waxhaw. Two days we'll be in Oconee County."

"Two days? Oh, praise the Lord." They'd been traveling for nearly a month. "I'm anxious for a real bed and a real bath."

"Our friend Cyrus was farming the land, and in return, he promised to keep up the house. He was a good, Godly man, so I expect things to be as they should…"

At the end, Ruth thought she heard a touch of doubt or concern in Noemie's voice. "But?"

"We got a letter from Cyrus once every few months, right up until the start of the war. Then nothing. I expect it's the war causing a disruption in the mail."

"Probably the day we left Silver Springs the post man delivered a dozen letters from him," Ruth said, trying to sound jocular.

Noemie did not laugh. Instead, she slowly set down her bowl, rose to her feet, and wandered over to the wagon. She draped an arm over the edge and stared intently into the darkness. Goosebumps dimpled Ruth's arms. "Is something amiss?"

"Helloooo, there at the fire."

A man's deep voice, thick with the syrup of a Southern accent, shocked Ruth to her feet. Noemie sliced the air with a hand, cut her eyes at Ruth, implying she be still and quiet.

"Who be ye?" Noemie called, her own mountain accent thickening as it did when she was angry.

"I was passing by and saw your fire. I haven't eaten in a few days." He paused, as if waiting for an invitation. Noemie did not issue one, surprising Ruth. "Could you spare anything?" The voice was closer, just outside the range of the low light.

"We've no extra. Move on," Noemie said firmly.

The young pines on the edge of their campsite moved, and an instant later, a man appeared. He was tall, thin, but not emaciated, and his clothes, though worn, were not ragged. If he was a deserter, he hadn't been on the run long. He held his hands out to his side, showing his empty palms. "You ain't very neighborly."

"You ain't very honest," Noemie retorted. "You were following us. I saw you back in Waxhaw. You noticed the girl. I noticed you."

The man grinned and dropped his hands. "Well, I thought maybe you two might..." he reached for something behind his back.

Instantly, Noemie snatched her shotgun from the wagon and leveled it on their guest, cocking both hammers. Ruth gasped. The man's eyes bugged, and he froze. "Nice and slow," Noemie barked. "What you got there?"

He gulped and produced a flask of liquid, most likely whiskey. "I ju—just thought—"

"You thought wrong, and it nearly cost you your head. Still might." She pressed the firearm a little tighter into her shoulder. "I see you again, I'm gonna assume you mean us harm."

Ruth could barely breathe, her heart was pounding so hard in her chest. Had the man come into their camp thinking to hurt them?

His eyes darted back and forth between the two of them and he shook his head. "It sure ain't worth this." He began to tremble, sending the liquor swirling in the bottle. "You're alone. I just thought—"

"Stop saying that," Noemie cut him off impatiently. "Get out of here. And don't come back. You've been warned."

The man huffed a breath and practically dove back into the woods. Ruth listened intently for several seconds until the sound of his thrashing faded completely. Noemie still held the gun at her shoulder, and her eyes were darting around the little clearing. Ruth decided not to move or relax until she did.

Several breaths later, Noemie released the hammers on her shotgun and leaned it carefully against the wagon. She picked up her stew and began eating again but remained standing.

Ruth's heart was just now slowing its thunderous pace. "Would—would you have shot him?"

"Faster than a fly can flick his wings."

Ruth didn't know what to make of this situation, or this new side to her mother-in-law. While she had always suspected a quiet strength in her, Noemie had suddenly turned into a fire-breathing hellion. Ruth was flummoxed by the woman's eagerness to not only mistrust the man but to resort to violence. Was this a manifestation of her grief? Would it pass or get worse?

"You wondering about my conduct?" she asked, her spoon clattering against her bowl.

"Yes," Ruth said hesitantly.

"Well, could be I am a mite testy lately. Running short on patience, shaking my fist at the Lord." She swallowed, shook her head. "That's part of it, but I saw that man back in town. He was awfully interested in us—in you. He had a Bowie knife in his back, not just a flask. I believe his intention was to rob us. I hope that was all."

Ruth glanced at the wagon. Noemie had a bag of gold hidden beneath the boards. The man may not have ever found it, but Ruth's reticule also had a few hundred dollars in it. She supposed two women alone, packed as if traveling a long distance, did look like they might have something to steal.

"I was afraid," Noemie continued, "city life might have made me a touch dull. Reckon I ain't as dull as I feared."

Ruth studied her mother-in-law casually tilting the bowl to her lips for the last of the broth. She wondered at the woman's steel. Her courage. And she pondered just who would be taking care of whom in Oconee County.

———

"I HAVE a sister down in Greenville who's been a widow for two years now. She's rather comely, if I do say so myself."

Montgomery Boaze stopped the glass of water at his lips and forced a smile for Mayor Fowler across the table. The man beamed with pride. And avarice. "I'm sure she is," Montgomery said politely, but he was thinking, *Then why isn't she married?* He finished his sip and set the glass down. "Well, I'd best be going." *Before you can tell me about her dowry.*

"Don't rush off. There will be dancing out on the lawn in just a little while."

All the more reason to hurry. Montgomery set the napkin on his plate. Nodded at the five other dinner guests at the table. "Farmers don't have the luxury of staying up late."

Fowler twirled his ridiculously long, red mustache. "You spend a lot of time alone, Montgomery. As your friend, I'm only trying to encourage you—"

"Thank you, Mayor."

"Don't worry about Montgomery there."

A slurred voice, raspy with alcohol, grated across Montgomery's nerves like a bow on an out-of-tune fiddle.

Leroy Heyward.

"He's got himself one handsome housekeeper. I imagine Darla's keeping his pillows fluffed—"

Montgomery slammed his hand down on the table, rattling every dish. The surge of anger surprised even him. "That'll be enough out of you, Heyward." The jaws of both men and women dropped as Montgomery rose to his feet, all six feet, six inches of him. At the opposite end of the table, Leroy matched his movement, and very nearly his height. Two big men, movers and shakers in the community. Only tonight, Heyward was moving from the alcohol, swaying like the ill-tempered drunk he was, glaring out from bloodshot eyes.

Montgomery easily imagined his knuckles crashing into Heyward's jaw, the crunch of bone ringing loud as his head snapped back. "I will not allow you to smear a fine, upstanding woman like Darla with lies."

Mayor Fowler stood, his eyes wide with fear. "It's the alcohol. I apologize for my guest, Montgomery. Leroy doesn't know what he's saying." The mayor glared right back at the man, commanding him with the stare to shut his mouth.

Leroy picked up his wine glass, swirled it sloppily, and grinned at Montgomery, a hint of mischief in his expression. He passed a hand over his graying, slicked-back hair. "My apologies. Darla is a woman with high standards." His expression soured. "She made it abundantly clear to me I still don't meet them...but you do."

Montgomery ground his teeth. The mere hint of impropriety with Darla—a lovely woman, but ten years his senior—would set tongues to wagging in Walhalla. And she'd done nothing to deserve a besmirched reputation. "Out of respect for the mayor and his company, Leroy, I'll walk away from this. But if I learn you've continued with this disrespect for Darla, I will put you flat on your back."

The two men held each other's gazes. The silence at the table was pristine. No one spoke. No one even blinked. Finally, Leroy waved his glass in subtle surrender. Montgomery sneered, furious at the man's behavior. So angry he feared he couldn't speak without spitting flames, he nodded abruptly to the guests and stormed from the room.

CHAPTER TWO

Noemie tugged the reins and brought the wagon to a stop. She stared down the sleepy, dusty main thoroughfare of the town and tears pooled in her eyes. Ruth reached out and touched her arm above the black band of mourning they both wore. "Are we home?"

Noemie nodded and gave her a sheepish grin. "Home. Walhalla." She cleared her throat and sniffled. "Well, let's make a quick stop at the mercantile here." She motioned to Fowler's Market on their right, a whitewashed building with a false front and boxes of fruit and vegetables displayed on the portico. "Get a few things, and maybe the lay of the land." She touched the braids winding around her head, as if making sure she looked presentable, and then jumped down.

Ruth eagerly unloaded and followed her mother-in-law into the dim store. Well-worn boards squeaked beneath her feet as she looked around. Several customers ambled about but stopped and looked the two newcomers over with suspicion. Beside her, Noemie grunted, as if disapproving of the open stares, and marched up to the counter.

A young man was tallying up the total for a grocery list. He straightened and made little effort to hide his own suspicion. "You new in town?"

Noemie grunted again. "Yes and no."

"Gotta see your papers, then."

"Papers?"

"All the residents have to have a permit showing they live in town."

"Why in the world?"

"Just tryin' to keep the deserters out."

"Do I look like a deserter, son?" Noemie narrowed her eyes at the boy and leaned in a little closer. "Say, you remind me of the Bryson family. You wouldn't be Mabel's boy, would you?"

He brightened instantly. "I am. I'm Willy."

"Lord, you were only about ten or so when James and me left. You've grown."

The boy's cheeks flushed. "Yes, ma'am."

"Ruth, this is Willy Bryson. His momma Mabel is my cousin." The two shook hands. "How is your momma?"

"Oh, she's fine, just fine. What are you doing back in these parts?"

"Come to spend my last years on the home place. I've missed my foothills something awful."

The boy's forehead scrunched. "Which is your place?"

"The farm at Frying Pan Ridge. Cyrus has been keeping it up for us. Reckon it'll need a lot of cleaning, but we'll look it over before—"

"Cyrus passed away, ma'am. Leroy Heyward's been running cattle on the place. Says he owns it. If we're speaking of the same farm."

Noemie's mouth dropped open. Ruth realized hers was agape as well and snapped it shut.

"Cyrus passed? How long ago? What happened?"

"He was out at Heyward's place—er, uh, or yours—dropped dead in the field. Doc figured a heart attack. Though he couldn't be sure. Poor Cyrus laid there for a few days."

Noemie sucked in a deep breath and stepped back. "How long ago? About two years?"

"Two or three, yes, ma'am. It was in the spring, is all I remember."

Noemie asked slowly, "And Leroy Heyward, you say, has been using the land?" Ruth heard the chill in the woman's tone. Obviously, there was no love lost between the two.

Willy's eyes widened with concern, as if he'd over-stepped, said too much. He nodded curtly.

A flinty edge settled on Noemie's face, hardening her expression, but, oddly, taking years from her face. The potential for trouble seemed to invigorate her. And worry Ruth.

"Let's check on the farm, girl." She pivoted and marched toward the door, Ruth hurrying behind her, praying nothing was seriously amiss with the home place, or who owned it.

————

THE HOUSE on Frying Pan Ridge had a long, dirt driveway that wound gently between two lush, green pastures—pastures full of someone's cattle. And even from this distance, Ruth could see that the two-story farmhouse was a mess. They rode toward it, and with every foot closer, her spirits sank.

Shutters hung askew, weeds and briars overgrew the yard, a tree had fallen on the roof, damaging the cedar shingles on the porch and at the chimney. A large branch had somehow slipped under the porch roof and shattered a kitchen window.

Further surveying revealed the hen house was empty, and the boards around the chicken run were sagging and rotting. As they rode up to the house, a squirrel dashed across the porch and dove into the bushes.

"Well, if this ain't somethin'," Noemie muttered. Anger and disappointment rolled off her in waves. "I expected messy, unkempt, but this..." Her gaze scanned the house, the outbuildings. "This'll be a project."

Oh, Lord, Ruth prayed, *help us. Don't let this be as bad as it looks.* "At least we have a roof over our heads," she reminded them both. The flicker of gratitude comforted her. There was much disappointment in this mess, but she needed to point out the lighter side for Noemie's sake. "And, yes, it'll be work. It's not what we expected, but it was a beautiful place...and it will be again."

Noemie clenched her jaw, scowled, then nodded. "You're right." She relaxed and took a deep breath. "It ain't wonderful, but it sure could be a whole lot worse. It could have burned to the ground." She set the brake. "Let's take a gander at the inside."

———

To Ruth's great relief, the interior of the house was only dusty and filled with cobwebs. The furniture had been draped with cloths. It didn't look as if anyone had been inside in years. Noemie drifted around the downstairs slowly, thoughtfully, touching end tables and covered portraits on the walls.

Her eyes again brimmed with tears, but she blinked them back. "Luke's family owned this farm. Passed it on to him. We had a good life here till he died. Lots of memories." She sighed. "Better check on the kitchen."

It turned out to be the one room with substantial damage. The tree had torn enough of the shingles loose that a major leak had developed between the ceiling and the stone chimney. Water had run down the back of the river rock fireplace—which served as the dividing wall between the living room and the kitchen—and rotted a spot in the floor near the stove. A branch from the tree had shattered the window at the breakfast nook, creating a hole that had allowed in more water, warping both the window casing and the small table that sat in the opening. Dirt, glass, debris, and dead bugs covered everything in the kitchen.

Ruth checked the stove, snatching the door open and stepping back. Layered in cobwebs and insect bodies, it at least didn't harbor any raccoons or snakes. Merely needed a good cleaning.

Noemie rested a hand on the river rock and stared at the mess. The dark, angry expression on her face, however, implied she was seeing more than the destruction in front of her.

The bellowing of a bull outside snapped the woman out of her deep and mysterious ruminations. She straightened and cut her eyes at Ruth. "I'm going into town. I'm gonna find Leroy—"

"Ye think that's a good idea?" Ruth certainly didn't think so. "Shouldn't ye find the sheriff first or—?"

"These are my people, Ruth. A lot of them are kin. I'll find out what's what before I see him, but I will see him. Today."

"Ye'll let me go with you." It wasn't a question.

Noemie looked around the kitchen, wandered out to the porch, strewn with wind-scattered leaves and pine boughs. "Maybe you could chop some wood and get the stove going for supper. Sweep up a little. I'll be back in time to eat."

Ruth's shoulders drooped at the wall Noemie was building. The woman was on a mission and had to complete it alone. Ruth felt shut out but tried to understand that there were things here she was not a part of. "I'll bring in some things from the wagon as well, then."

———————

MONTGOMERY TRIED to concentrate on the spring sun beating down on his shoulders as he drove his wagon toward town. Or the smell of honeysuckle in the air. The blue mountains off in the distance tempted him to climb higher and catch some rainbow trout from a bubbling creek.

He kept circling back around, though, to the cross words he'd had with Heyward last night. The man took every opportunity to challenge Montgomery, to try and best him at anything from farming to ranching to square dancing. And then, at the mayor's, to imply he had an inappropriate relationship with Darla. The foul accusation rankled Montgomery good, considering what a God-fearing woman she was.

Montgomery's hands tightened on the reins. *What is he, in his fifties? Acts more like a spoiled ten-year-old. Lord, forgive me, but that's the closest I've come yet to beating on him. Smearing the woman's reputation with rumor and innuendo. He has no manners. No morals.*

Montgomery feared he would soon have to school Leroy in at least some etiquette—a shameful thing, especially considering Leroy was probably a decade older. "I'm getting long in the tooth to be scrapping," he said aloud. "But, being in my forties doesn't mean I've got one foot in the grave, either. He speaks like that again about Darla, I will lay him out."

Two men of our years and standing in the community scuffling like children... ridiculous.

"I want to respect my elders, but he vexes me, Lord, purposely. I'm practicing the patience of Job, but can't promise that I'll succeed."

He topped the ridge and paused for a moment to drink in the view he saw every trip into Walhalla. The old Grant Place. A green, rolling valley of Southern pines and hardwoods budding fresh with the spring outlined dozens of rolling pastures filled with fences, cattle, and down by the river, a fallow field waiting for corn.

He frowned. He'd love to plant there if Heyward wasn't going to use it, but to lease land from the man was a revolting idea. Still, such a waste.

He sighed and moved to flick the reins when movement down at the old house caught his eye. At first, he assumed one of Heyward's men was working about the poor, neglected place, but it only took an instant for his eye to register curves. Definite, unmistakable curves. Montgomery squinted and leaned forward for a clarifying look.

Yes, a woman in a floppy hat and flowing blue skirt was chopping wood. *Now, who might that be?* He wondered. He'd heard no talk of Heyward moving to the place or leasing it.

Curiosity getting the better of him, he turned his horse from the main road and headed toward the stranger.

————

THE WOMAN REARED back with the axe to split a log, but suddenly brought the tool to her breast and spun to face Montgomery. He pulled the reins up as much to stop the horse as out of surprise. Dark, chocolate eyes gazed up at him from a pretty face all a-flush from the exertion of her work. A long braid of hair the color of molasses hung over her shoulder. She was trim, shapely, alluring, and he caught himself thinking, *If I were a younger man...*

Her surprise quickly melted away, replaced with suspicion and then fear. That jolted Montgomery out of his pitiful rudeness. "Good afternoon, I'm Montgomery Boaze. Who might you be?"

"Why is that any of yer concern?"

He almost smiled at her melodic, Irish brogue. The lady was a long way from home. Then he frowned because the answer wouldn't put him in the best light. "Well, Leroy Heyward owns this place, and you don't look like Leroy. I'll confess that curiosity got the better of me."

The axe lowered a little, but apparently so she could twist for a better grip. "Are you a friend of this Mr. Heyward?"

Montgomery really hated to answer the question, but lying wasn't an option. "I'm afraid I'm a lot of things to Leroy Heyward. A friend isn't one of them."

"Ye say he owns this place. My mother-in-law, Noemie Grant, begs to differ."

Simultaneously, Montgomery caught the *in-law* part, implying the young lady was married, and the name.

"Noemie Grant? She's back in Oconee County?" Montgomery recovered quickly from the unexpected disappointment. "I haven't seen Noemie in ten years or more." He started looking around for her. "Where is she?" He locked the brake and moved to step down when the girl raised the axe, positioning for a swing.

"Hold it right there. I don't know ye. I don't know yer intentions. Stay in the wagon."

Montgomery settled back into the seat and spoke calmly. "Get Noemie. She'll know me. I'm her kin."

"She's not here." The girl flinched as if she shouldn't have revealed the information. "She'll be back any minute, though."

"You've no need to be afraid of me, ma'am. You can put the axe down."

"I'll decide that."

Montgomery pondered things a moment, then circled back around to Heyward. Seemed he was a thorn of some sort for everyone. "You say Noemie still owns this place?"

"Aye. She had a caretaker forever until—"

"Cyrus. Yes, he passed away a few years ago and Heyward told everyone he bought this place."

"Well, I don't know the man. I won't cast aspersions on his character. All I know is Noemie went looking for him " — the axe slipped a little— "and I wish she hadn't. She's angry and likely will spout off without thought."

"Well, Heyward's a braggart and a loud-mouthed tyrant, but he won't hurt a woman."

"You misunderstand. I fear for this Mr. Heyward. Noemie left with her shotgun by her side."

Montgomery leaned back and chewed on his bottom lip a second. "Hmm. She always did have a fiery temper."

"It's worse now. Her son, my husband James, was killed

at Leesburg. Little more than a year before that, her husband passed. I fear she's lost what self-control she might have had."

Montgomery picked up the reins. "I'll see if I can find her. Before she finds Heyward." The girl moved as if she wanted to say something but bit it back. Montgomery took a chance. "Would you want to come with me?" he asked, hesitantly. "You can keep your axe."

It only took her a moment. "Yes. I would." She hurried over to the wagon and climbed up. Settling, she pinned Montgomery with a firm gaze, showing her fear as well as her determination. "I'm Ruth Grant, and Noemie's all I have in the world."

Montgomery nodded and offered his hand. "I'm Montgomery Boaze."

CHAPTER THREE

Ruth's immediate reaction to Montgomery Boaze was not fear, but of course the memory of the stranger invading their camp sprang up in her mind like a weed. She second-guessed the wisdom now of being in the wagon with this man. Making no secret of her assessment, she scrutinized him top to bottom.

His white shirt, sleeves rolled up to his elbows, and worn, brown suspenders bespoke a man who jumped into work. He had a handsome face weathered by his years, the crow's feet emphasizing seasoned good looks. His beard, streaked with silver, was in need of a trim. Wavy, brown hair, touched with gray at the temples, grazed his collar. *He could use a barber*, she thought, *but aye, he's not dangerous.*

A sincere smile lifted the corner of his mouth. "You really are safe with me, Mrs. Grant. I'm a gentleman...not to mention, probably old enough to be your father."

His gentle, slightly gravelly voice and the humor in it worked a grin from her. "If ye started about twelve or fifteen. I'm not usually so jittery of strangers, but we met a bad element a few nights back."

"Did you and Noemie travel alone all the way from... Maryland, was it?"

She noted his forearms, strong and solid, and tanned by the sun. "Aye, and the trip was fine until that one incident. Thank God it was the only one. Noemie was quite literally prepared to shoot a man to protect me. Us."

"She always was a momma bear. I remember once she ran a mountain lion off the place. It had been stalking James."

Ruth had no doubt. And, yes, in hindsight, protectiveness had brought out the cool ruthlessness in her mother-in-law. A wild and fierce woman she'd become in that moment. "She's a force to be reckoned with."

They rode in silence for a moment before he cut his eyes at Ruth, and she saw they were a stunning blue. "I'd be willing to bet you are, as well. I'm sorry about James." His expression turned angry. "Lot of good boys dying for a poor cause."

Grief and guilt bubbled up in her and she sighed, trying to exhale them. "Aye," was all she could manage.

"How long were you married?"

"Five years. I was twenty-three when we met. I'd only just come to America and had taken work at a shipping company. I'm quite good with figures, and Mr. Grant gave me a chance. I met James in the office."

"Married the boss's son? That must have caused quite a stir."

"I think normally it would have, but we courted two years before we were married."

"A man of propriety and patience."

"Yes, he was. And it was important to him that Noemie

like me." She frowned. It had been *very* important to him, almost as if he'd known his mother might end up alone.

"Well, it sounds as if she may have lost a son but gained a daughter." Mr. Boaze smiled at Ruth, and the warmth in his gaze calmed her even more. A handsome man for his years, and almost fatherly...almost. But he did have a steadying effect on her, as if she knew instinctively he was a man to be trusted, a secure, reliable man.

"What is it that you do, Mr. Boaze?"

"I'm a farmer. And I tell you, I hope it's true that Noemie still owns her place. She's got some land I'd like to lease for a crop of corn."

"I guess we will see what happens when she finds Mr. Heyward."

———

"Preacher," Noemie called, peeking into the sanctuary of the First Baptist Church. "Kenneth, you in here?" The empty pews answered with silence.

She marched around back to the parsonage and found Reverend Harmon in his vegetable garden, weeding his squash. He was a little older than Noemie and had gained some weight and a smattering of gray hair in the preceding decade. Still, she would have known him anywhere. The man had been her first heartbreak...a hundred years ago. Tall, still muscular, with close-cropped chestnut hair, he had, overall, aged quite nicely.

She checked the braids wound around her head for loose hairs and swallowed. "Kenneth," she tried again softly, and he looked up. "You remember me?"

Comprehension dawned in his eyes and he climbed nimbly to his feet. "Noemie? Lord! Well, I'll be." He stepped over his lettuce and gave her a big hug. "Of course, I remember you. A man, even one of the cloth, never forgets his first kiss."

Remarkably, Noemie felt her cheeks warm. She wondered how long it had been since she'd blushed. "You remember that, huh?"

He threw back his head and laughed with great delight. "I'll say." He dropped an arm around her with relaxed familiarity and led her over to a bench beneath an oak. "I'm tickled to see you back in Walhalla."

"It's good to be back."

"Momma's still with us. You'll have to pay her a call."

They sat, turned slightly toward one another, and she found his gaze oddly intense. For the first time in years, she felt awkward. "I will do that. Miss Viola is one of my favorite people. What of your pa?"

"He went home to be with the Lord, oh, I guess it's been five years now. He had a good run and finished up at eighty-seven."

"Willard always had a smile for me. I'm sorry for your loss."

Kenneth waved a hand, accepting the condolences, and nodding at her black arm band. "So, is this a social call or... I see you've lost someone."

"My son, James. Battle of Leesburg."

"I'm sorry."

"Damnable war." She flinched at the curse word she'd let slip.

He nodded slightly. "I agree. It is damnable. An event straight from hell." He patted her hand. "How can I help?"

"Tell me what's going on with my home place."

His brow dove. "I'm not sure I understand the question."

"What's Heyward doing on it?"

Suspicion alighted on the preacher's handsome, bearded face. "He's told everyone he bought it from you, after Cyrus's passing. Your question leads me to believe that may not be the case."

"Isn't the case. Isn't the truth." An ember of fury was growing in Noemie. She'd never liked Heyward. She remembered him as a petulant, dishonest, greedy opportunist. "Tell me something, Kenneth."

"What's that?"

"Is Leroy Heyward still the conniving, self-serving, crooked snake he was when I left?"

"Nope."

Noemie relaxed a little.

"He's worse."

Her fingers curled into fists. "So, most likely he thought I wouldn't come back, and he'd just take my property."

"Claim squatter's rights?"

"He has no rights." Noemie shot to her feet. "I'll see you later, Kenneth. Maybe Sunday."

He rose and chased after her. "You seem perturbed, Noemie. I remember your temper. Mightn't you like to get the sheriff to help you with this? You'd be more commanding with the law behind you."

Noemie stopped abruptly and cut her eyes to him. He inched back. "Oh, I'm quite sure I'll have no trouble commanding his attention." If she didn't shoot him the moment she saw him.

———

SOMETIMES LEROY HEYWARD felt like worms were squirming in his brain. He stabbed the steak on the plate before him and sawed off a piece. Around him, plates and silverware clinked. Chatter flowed through the restaurant with a grating hum.

He had too much going on. He needed more peace and quiet than this to do some thinking. A shipment of cattle was coming in today...140 bales of cotton were sitting at the station in Greenville...Zeb Buchanan had not delivered on his promise of two prize hogs. The mayor was diddling about the town slave ordinance—

"Noemie Grant. Willy saw her just today."

The woman's voice stopped the fork midway to Leroy's mouth. A sliver of fear coursed through him and he swore silently. *What in tarnation is she doing back—?*

"My lands," another woman replied. "She's been gone forever. Wonder what she's doing here."

"Well, that's the funny thing," Mabel Bryson—Leroy recognized her voice now—dropped her volume to a whisper. "Willy said Noemie seemed completely flustered to find out Leroy Heyward said he owned the farm."

"What in the world?"

Leroy set down his fork. If Noemie was back, he had a problem. The click of the hammer on a shotgun as it pressed against the back of his head convinced him he was right. Café patrons gasped as one.

"Leroy Heyward."

Sweat beaded on his upper lip and suddenly his armpits felt clammy. He swore silently. "That you, Noemie?" He didn't quite succeed in keeping a warble from his voice.

"You know doggone well it's me." The shotgun barrel tapped him hard in the skull, then Noemie stepped around in front of him, still holding the business end of the scatter gun trained on him. "You snake. You sniveling, lying, sneaking piece of white trash. Why in the world did you think I wouldn't find out?"

Because you weren't supposed to come back to this rat hole! No one ever does.

"I don't know what you're talking about, cousin. And that is one heck of a way to greet family." He motioned to the barrel. "I see being north of the Mason-Dixon hasn't improved your disposition any." All five feet of his little cousin was wound as tight as the braids around her head.

"Maybe not, but it also didn't make me stupid. You've got some nerve just waltzing on to my place."

An evil idea struck Leroy, and he hoped it would buy him some time. "You're crazy, or as confused as an old, blind hound. You sold me your place and you know it."

Noemie sneered at him. "I didn't sell you nothing. Especially my farm."

Leroy skipped glances over the dozen or so wide-eyed folks in the café . "That's it. She's crazy. Crazy as a bed bug. Look at her, all wild-eyed and pointing a scatter gun at me. You always did have a shingle loose, Cousin Noemie." He started to rise. "Why don't we take this outside?" *Where I can throttle you.*

"Sit down," Noemie bellowed, raising the shotgun to the ceiling. The gun roared and wood rained down over their heads. Men gasped. Women screamed. They all hunkered down in fear, hands over their ears. Before Leroy could speak, the barrel was trained on him again. "As you've probably gathered, I'm a mite perturbed at your behavior."

"Cousin Noemie. " He swallowed the pleading tone in his voice, tried to think through the ringing in his ears. "There's some confusion here." Was she really going to kill him? Had the woman lost her mind for real? He didn't want to risk annoying her further, but he had to get out of this. "I didn't steal your farm. I bought it." He spoke softly, as if addressing a daft child holding a stick of dynamite and a match. "You sold it to me. It's been a couple of years. Maybe you've just forgotten."

The woman tensed up like she might fire the second barrel and Leroy flinched, but she controlled herself. "I'm not dead, Leroy. I have my faculties." She pulled back the trigger on the second barrel. "Call me crazy again."

Nope. No way. Leroy wasn't going to answer the challenge. He was keenly aware that his life might actually be hanging by a thread.

"Noemie Grant."

Montgomery Boaze's voice brought a glimmer of hope to Leroy that the thread had just gotten a little stronger.

"You're not back a full day and look at the trouble you're causing."

Noemie huffed a disgusted breath but didn't look at the man standing behind her. "He stole my farm," she said flatly.

"I didn't steal anything," Leroy said, regaining some calm.

"Noemie, please." A pretty girl with what sounded like an Irish accent stepped up to the woman and looked at her. Noemie didn't budge. She just kept that glare trained on Leroy, green eyes burning hot with trouble. The girl raised her hand as if to touch the barrel but stopped just short. "This is no way to get things done. We'll go to the law."

No, that solution wouldn't work any better, Leroy acknowledged. He rubbed his neck, the muscles tighter than the grimace on Noemie's face, then he opened his hands to her. "Give me a chance to explain. Outside."

No one moved. No one breathed. The ticking of the

Regulator clock on the wall counted off the seconds. Abruptly, Noemie folded the shotgun across her chest. "Fine." Fifteen people exhaled at the same time. "Cousin Witlow."

A bald man rose up behind the batwings separating the dining room from the kitchen. He gulped and nodded. "Y-yes, Cousin Noemie."

"Figured you still run the place. Sorry for the damage. I'll pay for it." She spun on her heel, her skirt swirling like a twister around her ankles. "Outside, Leroy."

He exhaled a long, relieved breath, but stopped it short when he caught Montgomery looking at him. *Always so high-and-mighty,* he thought. *Can't do anything wrong. Everything he touches turns to gold. Well, my turn is coming, Boaze. Watch and see.*

———

MONTGOMERY EXCHANGED a concerned glance with Ruth as they followed Noemie outside. She was still cradling the shotgun and he gave some thought to taking it from her but decided against it. "Noemie, I'm surprised at you." He hated to scold the woman, but honestly, what was going on in her head? "You think that's the way to handle Heyward?"

An impish grin lit on her little mouth and she wiggled her eyebrows. "Watch and see."

A moment later, Leroy joined them, moving gingerly, his hands up, his gaze glued to the shotgun. "We're going to the courthouse," she told him. "I'll see this deed I must have signed."

"Now, I don't think we need to go to all that trouble." Hayward, a muscular man who Montgomery suspected was not as nervous as he looked, pulled a handkerchief from his back pocket and dabbed at the sweat on his forehead. "Why are you back, anyway? I thought you'd spend the rest of your life up in Maryland with your husband."

"Yeah, I guess that is what you thought. Well, my second husband is dead, Leroy, and now so is James. Battle of Leesburg." Her tone was sharp, impatient. "I came back because this is my home. My people. My roots."

Leroy deflated and pursed his lips. He ran a hand over his thinning, slick-backed hair. "I'm sorry, Cousin. I had no idea, of course. Listen, I'm sure we can fix this, somehow. I wouldn't turn you out."

"Turn me out?" Noemie looked as if she couldn't believe the idea. "From my own farm?"

Leroy shoved his hands into his pockets and rocked on his heels. He reminded Montgomery of a frog on a grill, and he wanted off. "You know, I'm doing very well now. Just ask Montgomery here. I'm his biggest competition in the Upstate. I don't think he out- farms me by about, what, a hundred acres?"

"I didn't know it was a competition, Leroy."

"There is no deed, is there? You're a squatter. Just say it." Noemie screwed her face up into a tight grimace of indignation that was almost fierce.

"Well, uh," Leroy cleared his throat and ducked his chin at Noemie. "Let's not get tripped up on details. I can afford to let you have your place back—"

"Back?" She nearly choked on the word and Montgomery elbowed her lightly. He didn't know what Leroy was up to, but for the moment thought they should go along.

"Leroy, you've made use of your cousin's land here with

no expenses," Montgomery said calmly. "Now that she's a widow, I should think you'd want to offer some remuneration to her."

"Remun...er..." Leroy trailed off, looking bewildered.

He was a big man, savvy, but not educated. "Pay her back-rent," Montgomery explained.

Fire flared in the man's eyes, and for a moment, Montgomery thought Leroy might try to choke him for the suggestion. He settled back quickly, however, glancing around the street. He didn't seem to want a scene. Which, after the public shouting match he'd dragged Montgomery into over Darla the night before, this behavior puzzled him. Maybe he needed liquor to get mouthy.

"Fine. Remuneration. I reckon that's fair."

Noemie narrowed her eyes at Leroy. "You've got cattle on my property. I want 'em off by sundown."

Leroy scowled at the woman and worked his broad jaw back and forth. Finally, after several seconds, he nodded. "All right. Mighty unfriendly of you, but all right." Lips a tight, angry line, he nodded once more and strode off, muttering underneath his breath.

"I just had to scare him," Noemie said after a minute. She winked at Ruth. "He always scared easy as a kid. Backed out of everything we tried to do if it had a whiff of danger. Rope swings, tree houses, playing with his pa's dynamite. He always gave in to fear and ran like the scalded cur he is."

"Noemie," Montgomery shifted to stand directly in front of the little woman who barely came to his shoulders. "I'm taking you to task for what you did in there. Every tongue in Walhalla is going to be wagging over this. Everybody is going to think you're—"

"Crazy? Good. They'll leave me alone then." She hugged the shotgun tighter and stared off into the distance, a petulant tilt to her head.

"Crazy with grief, I was going to say. And people will forgive that. But don't push them too far."

"I got my farm back. That's all that matters." She looked up at Montgomery and flashed a saucy smile, one that had devastated a few men in town in years past. Or so he'd heard. "But I do apologize to you. This was no way to greet a cousin."

Ruth's pretty, chocolate eyes bugged. "He's your cousin, too?"

"Far removed," Montgomery said too quickly.

One of Noemie's eyebrows ticked up. "Fifth, once removed, if I recall."

Montgomery resisted the urge to shift his feet or look away. She lowered the shotgun barrel to point at the ground and reached out for a hug. Relaxing a little, he hugged her back.

"My, you've grown," she said. "In the middle."

Montgomery tapped his stomach. "The years have put some weight on me." For some reason, he watched Ruth to see her reaction to his middle-aged paunch. She merely smiled pleasantly.

"Didn't hurt your looks none. Always were a handsome man. How's Maddie Sue?" Montgomery's expression answered before he had a chance to rein it in and she pursed her lips. "Not so good, I guess."

"I lost her five years ago to tick fever." Montgomery clenched his teeth, pushing away the image of his wife, bathed in sweat, taking her last breath in his arms. "Bryl is at West Point. He turned out all right, despite me raising him alone for too much of his life."

Noemie squeezed his forearm. "I'm sure he couldn't have had better leading." She took a deep breath and turned to Ruth. "How did you two happen upon each other?"

"He came by the farm—"

"I was sticking my nose in where it didn't belong," he said sheepishly. "I saw somebody at the house and got curious."

Noemie scrunched up her face, as if debating the truth of his statement, then chuckled. "Reckon I'm glad you did. It's good to see you, boy."

"The house is a wreck. You two have your work cut out for you. I'll send some hands over—"

"Now, you don't have to—" Noemi started to protest, but for some reason bit it off. "Might could use the help, at that. The kitchen is a pretty mess. Got a tree l ying across it."

"Water damage?"

"Around the chimney."

"Hmmm." Montgomery would remind himself to send Caleb Jones. He was a good carpenter.

"Why don't you come by tomorrow, Montgomery?" Noemie's tone changed, sweetened. She even batted her eyelashes. "I'll walk you around the house and you can give two helpless females some ideas on how to tackle the mess."

He squinted at his cousin, her tone ringing warning bells. "You don't have to sweet- talk me, Noemie. I offered the help." But surveying the damage probably wasn't a bad idea, and he acquiesced. "I could come by tomorrow."

"We could feed ye lunch for yer trouble," Ruth offered politely.

Montgomery didn't read anything into it, but he liked

the idea, maybe not for the most selfless reasons. It'd been some time since he'd been in the company of a young, pretty female. His housekeeper Darla was kind and helpful, beautiful, to boot, but older than Noemie. "I'll be there at noon."

CHAPTER FOUR

Ruth glanced over her shoulder as Noemie slapped the reins across the horse's back. The wagon was full of some basic supplies—coffee, sugar, bacon, and the like—along with tools for cleaning this and fixing that. A tremendous amount of hard work lay ahead, but she was excited to get to it. The chores would keep her and Noemie busy. It would be good for them both.

"So, what do you think? " Noemie asked without looking at her.

"About what?"

"Oh, about everything. Coming here. The farm. Montgomery."

Ruth thought perhaps there had been a slight pause before Montgomery's name, but she couldn't be sure. Surely her mother-in-law wasn't looking to pawn Ruth off on a stranger. Then again...

She cut her eyes at Noemie. The woman was concerned for her welfare. Ruth wouldn't put a little matchmaking past the woman. "I'm glad I'm here with you, Noemie. Mr.

Heyward has stepped out of the way and ye've yer farm back. It will be a lovely place when we're done with it, though I see a long summer of hard work. And what was the last part?" She fought a smile that threatened to give away her mischief.

"Montgomery. Just curious what you thought of him."

"Oh, he seems very nice. I think when ye're ready to marry again he'll be—"

"Marry?" Noemie's eyes nearly bugged out of her skull and Ruth had to look away. "He's ten years younger than me. At least."

"Aye, he's young, but he's strong and he seems kind."

"I was thinking more about you. You know, on down the road. When you're ready."

Ruth sighed and let the joke go. "Far down the road." How would she ever be able to tell Noemie she missed James, but not as deeply as she should? Ruth had lost a friend, one from whom she'd been drifting for a while. Unable to confess it, she changed the direction of the talk. "Besides, don't ye think Mr. Boaze is a bit old for me?"

Truthfully, his age—forty or so, she guessed—did not bother her. She had noticed the lines around his stunning sapphire eyes, but thought they gave him character. The gray at his temples blended nicely with his wavy chestnut hair, rounding out a wise-looking and handsome face. The slight thickening at his middle only served to create an air of steadiness, trustworthiness. He was probably fifteen years her senior, a noticeable gap, enough to where she could think of him in a fatherly way. Yet, she didn't.

"You'll have plenty of young men calling on you, Ruth, once this war is over. My advice is to give consideration to Montgomery. He's kind, wealthy, stable. He'd make a good husband."

"Even if I were to *give him consideration,* don't ye think ye're putting the cart before the horse? I've only just met the man."

"I reckon with Jeremiah and James both gone, I'm less inclined to make plans for my own future. Anything could happen to me. I just want you taken care of."

"Are ye worried about Mr. Heyward? I don't like the man. He gives me an uneasy feeling."

"Ah, maybe he's dangerous, but mostly he's just stupid."

"Don't ye think he acquiesced awfully easy to your and Mr. Boaze's demands? I got the feeling he was eager to avoid a scandal."

"He's a squatter and didn't want everyone in town to know it. 'Specially after he told them he bought the farm. That's my guess, anyway."

"He's pretending to have more money than he actually does?"

"I think so, and he wants to keep this little scandal just between us. Wish he would have at least put a little effort into upkeep while availing himself of my farm."

Ruth smiled and hooked an arm through Noemie's. "Together, we'll have the house ship-shape in no time."

"Did you get much done this afternoon?"

"Not as much as I'd hoped, of course, but I swept the kitchen clean and was chopping wood for the stove when Mr. Boaze came by. We can at least cook supper."

Noemie looked up at the sky. "We're running out of daylight. Let's have a cold supper and use the time to beat the mattresses and dust our rooms. I'm ready to sleep in a real bed again."

Yes, as was Ruth, but she had something else she was dreaming about. "Noemie, would ye think me vain and foolish if I said all I wanted was to sit in your plunge bathtub?"

The question seemed to stump the woman for a moment, then she burst out laughing. "Lord, have mercy, I'd forgotten about that thing. It was the first one in the county. My dear departed Luke bought it as a present for me, and it had folks in an uproar. They said he was trying to kill his new bride by giving her pneumonia."

Ruth giggled as well. "'Twas my favorite thing about our house in Maryland. I was grieving its loss."

"Well, you can take as long and as deep a plunge bath as you can boil water for."

As Noemie turned the wagon down the driveway, Ruth flicked a hand at the empty pasture. "The cattle are gone."

"Least he was smart enough to get them off my land and not dilly-dally." Noemie steered the horse toward the front porch and set the br ake. She paused, staring up at the forlorn home. The shadow of sadness clouded her other-wise still comely face, tugging at Ruth's heart.

She reached over and offered an encouraging hug. "Don't worry. It'll look like it should in no time. Now, aren't ye glad I came along?"

It took her a moment, but Noemie nodded. "I reckon it won't be quite so lonely after all."

———

BY THE TIME they had unloaded the wagon, lugged the mattresses outside for beating, pounded the dust from them, and then dragged them back upstairs, Ruth fell across Noemie's bed exhausted, but was stunned that the older woman was still standing. "I'm done in."

"As am I." Noemie grinned and lay down beside her.

"You say you still want a plunge bath, I'll do my best to help you heat the water and get it to the tub."

Oh, if only she could. "I think I've barely the strength to pour water into the basin and wipe off the dust."

The two women lay in companionable silence for a moment, and then Ruth heard the soft, gurgling sounds of Noemie's gentle snoring. Slowly, and with great effort, she sat up and looked around the room. Pieces of furniture, still hidden beneath their dust sheets, were vaguely eerie in the flickering lamplight. She and Noemie had managed to wrestle a trunk up here and it contained a few quilts. She retrieved one and laid it lightly across her mother-in-law's slender frame and then carefully raised her feet to the bed. She considered removing the woman's shoes, but Noemie rolled over and curled up into a tight, cozy ball, and Ruth relinquished the idea.

She lamented the fact they'd not had time to make the bed properly, but tomorrow was another day. With what little energy she had left, she took the lamp and made her way to the kitchen. Ruth was desperately tired but wanted to fill a pitcher with water and clean up a bit before retiring. If the ablution revived her, she might make her own bed. Otherwise, like Noemie, a quilt would have to do.

She set the lamp on the counter, dug through a box for a tin pitcher, and took it to the pump. So much work for such a little thing, but she wanted the day's grime off her. She pumped once, twice, and finally on the third try, a gush of water hit the pitcher. Once more, and she had enough to bathe with.

As she picked up the pitcher, she heard a soft shuffle from behind and whirled toward the damaged window. The tree had shattered the glass pane and the hole opened up to the inky darkness outside. Nothing moved. Yet, she felt as if someone...something...was staring back at her.

Her skin went cold.

A chorus of crickets accused her of foolishness. Still, she stared into the night, frozen. Something on the porch moved softly, almost stealthily. A sound so soft she could argue she hadn't heard it, but it caused her pulse to riot in fear. Her chest rose and fell with short, quick breathes.

"Is someone there?" A ridiculous question. Surely, a squirrel or a raccoon was knocking about, but...

The gooseflesh rising on her arms said differently. She set the pitcher down and raised the lamp overhead to keep the glare from her eyes. As her vision began to adjust, she thought she saw a shadow moving away from the broken windows. A man? Or a bear?

Fear threatened to seize her muscles. She waited, listened, craning to hear over the pounding in her chest.

A bear would have run most likely, but not without a snort or a grunt. This shadow had slipped away in silence. Could it have been Mr. Heyward? Or even Mr. Boaze?

Her idea of a bath gone, Ruth dashed to Noemie's room, softly closed and locked the door behind her, then surveyed the ghostly sheets. The legs of a rocking chair protruded from beneath one. Her heart beginning to resume something akin to a normal beat, she freed the chair and placed it next to the bed for a clear view of the door and sat. Quite sure sleep couldn't claim her now, she vowed to sit here, bolt upright, and watch over Noemie.

CHAPTER FIVE

RUTH'S EYES OPENED WIDE AND SHE SAT BOLT UPRIGHT, HER first thought was of the shadow at the broken window. Blinking away sleep, she looked around Noemie's room as the quilt on top of her slid to the floor. Noemie's bed was empty and the heavenly aroma of bacon drifted up from the kitchen. Evidently, exhaustion had overcome Ruth's fear. She was troubled by this as it made her feel vulnerable and foolish. Somehow, if the situation had been reversed, she doubted *Noemie* would have fallen asleep on guard duty.

"Ruth, you awake? Breakfast is ready," the woman called from downstairs.

Chagrined, disappointed in herself, Ruth rose and stretched. "Coming. Coming." Stiff in places she didn't believe possible, she moved slowly, trudging down the steps as she redid the messy braid in her hair. Noemie was urging two fried eggs onto a plate as Ruth stepped into the kitchen. "Why didn't ye wake me sooner?"

Noemie replaced the frying pan on the stove and sat

down, waving Ruth to join her. "You had a reason for sleeping in that rocker, I assumed." She poured them both coffee. "New house, noises and all, get to you?"

Ruth shifted her gaze to the shattered windows. Sunlight streamed in. She could see past the porch, over the weedy yard, to the barn and chicken coop. Beyond them, rolling hills and a ridge of mountains. It all looked so safe and inviting.

Noemie set her coffee down. "What is it? Something happen last night?"

"I—I…" A bear or a man? In the light of day, both possibilities seemed foolish. "I thought I saw something—someone—no, something on the porch last night."

Noemie studied the window intently.

"A shadow. Surely it was a bear or something of the like, or my nerves turned a raccoon into something taller."

"Maybe. Maybe not." Noemie reached out and squeezed Ruth's hand. "We'll look around after breakfast."

Both women made quick work of the bacon and eggs, cleaned up, and headed outside. Nothing obvious on the porch spoke of company—man or beast—but in the yard, partly overgrown with briars, Noemie plucked a tiny piece of frayed, blue-gray wool from a thorn. She raised it to eye level and examined it. "Don't reckon any bear wears wool."

"So, I did see someone?" Ruth's stomach rolled with fear.

"Leroy could have taken to spying. Wouldn't put it past him. Or maybe we've got a deserter on the premises. Stay right here."

Noemie disappeared into the house and returned a moment later with her shotgun.

"What are ye going to do with that?"

"We're looking for something. This is in case we find something. Let's start with the chicken coop."

They approached the poor, sway-backed structure with caution and stepped inside the fencing. Noemie motioned to the door. "Open it, but get out of the way."

Her pulse racing, sweat slicking her palms, Ruth grabbed hold of the door and tugged...and tugged again. Stuck fast. She grabbed it with both hands and gave it a mighty yank. She leaped out of the way, and Noemie raised the shotgun.

It was obvious, however, that no one had been in the coop for some time. A cloud of dust drifted from the shadowy opening. "Let's try the barn."

As they approached it, Noemie studied the ground. "I see our wagon tracks, reckon Montgomery's..." She peered closer at something, pointed at it with her toe. "Did Montgomery get out of the wagon when he was here?"

"No."

"Hmmmm." Noemie eyed the barn with suspicion and moved toward it. "Well, there's a few prints around, but they're too hard to read. Let's see if there's any boogeymen in the stall."

Shotgun pressed to her shoulder, Noemie stepped quietly into the barn, Ruth right behind her. The building was in better shape than the house, and it was mostly empty. Their horses still in the paddock outside, the three stalls in the barn were open and had been cleaned some time ago. A plow stood by itself at the far end of the aisle, in front of a wall hung with all the necessary tack. A wagon with one missing wheel rested on a jack.

No sign of company.

"Let's check the loft." Noemie reached down and pulled her skirt up between her legs, tucking it into her belt. At

Ruth's questioning gaze, the woman squared her shoulders. "Don't wanna shoot myself by tripping over my skirt."

Carefully, the two of them climbed up, Noemie easing her head up to the loft for a look around. Nothing apparently arresting her attention, she scrambled on up, Ruth on her heels. The loft was large, open, and stacked high with loose, golden hay. A ton of it, Ruth noted. Thick cobwebs implied no one had been up here in a while, either.

"Don't know about last night, but as of now, I think it's just you and me."

As if to argue, the jangling of a wagon announced company. Still cautious, Noemie kept the shotgun up as she and Ruth walked the narrow, clear path to the hay door and peered out. Montgomery looked up at them as he pulled back on the reins. "Mornin', ladies. I'm early. I hope that's all right. It worked out better for me."

"Morning, Montgomery. Leroy has left my loft full of good hay. I think I'll keep it and count it toward the remuneration you mentioned."

"I think that's fair. Especially considering he destroyed half your fence on Acorn Ridge moving his cattle out."

———

MONTGOMERY DRUMMED his fingers on his coffee cup and looked across the table at the two women, aware his face expressed his concern. "How sure are you of what you saw?"

Ruth lowered her head, a sheepish expression stealing across her pretty features. "In the light of day, I'm willing to admit perhaps I was merely tired. The shadows from the lantern could have played tricks on my eyes."

Most likely, she was right. Just a nervous female, alone

in the dark. Her nerves had gotten the better of her. "What do you think, Noemie?"

"I wouldn't put nothing past Leroy...but we didn't see any sign other than that itty-bitty piece of wool and maybe some prints." She shook her head. "Hard to say. But nobody's been in the coop for months, and the barn looked fairly untouched."

"We won't jump to any conclusions then, but keep your eyes open. Could have been a deserter passing through, maybe."

Noemie shrugged a shoulder. "No livestock on the place. Maybe he would have noted it and moved on."

"The more I think about it, the more foolish I feel. I've alarmed everyone and—"

"No," Montgomery interrupted. "Don't feel foolish. We've got more than our share of deserters. It's possible you did see someone."

"We'll not dwell on it, but we'll keep our eyes open," Noemie said.

Montgomery nodded, finished his coffee, then studied the broken window and the water-damaged floor by the fireplace. "That's going to take a fair amount of work to repair." His gaze drifted over the ceiling. "Have you checked the attic for leaks?"

Ruth and Noemie exchanged surprised and then guilty looks. "No," the older woman admitted. "Didn't even cross my mind."

"I say we look everything over, top to bottom, from the roof to the barn to the fence, and make a detailed list of what this place needs. Then you'll know what you're dealing with."

Two hours later, Montgomery and Noemie sat down on the front porch step, both of them dabbing at sweaty brows. Inspecting the sweltering attic, then assessing the fence, chicken coop, and barn in the direct sun and sticky air had reminded him he wasn't a strapping lad anymore. Ruth, on the other hand, merely had a pretty flush to her cheeks.

Hands on her hips, she surveyed the empty porch from the bottom step. Swept clean, but it was devoid of any furniture. "Why don't I make us some lunch?"

"Thank you, child," Noemie said. "And why don't you bring Montgomery a glass of water."

He started to rise. "I can get—"

"No, no," Ruth waved for him to sit. "You two cool off. I'll be right back."

She slipped between him and Noemie and he tried to ignore the pleasurable feel of her fingers on his shoulder. He turned his attention to the yard, overgrown with weeds and thistles. As was much of the farm. "Noemie, there's a lot of work to be done. To start with, I'll send my hand Bear over—"

"Bear?" She looked at Montgomery with obvious skepticism. "What kind of scallywag goes by the name of Bear?"

"A sixteen-year-old boy who's as big and thick as a black bear. And as strong. He'll be a big help to you."

"Oh, so the name fits?"

"He's mighty stout. He'll move, lift, or carry anything you can't yourselves." He turned on the step and eyed the damage to the kitchen, the tree still lying across the roof, some of its smaller branches protruding into the kitchen. "We'll start with that."

"Just one of a thousand tasks."

Montgomery heard the disgust in her voice. "Cyrus was

doing a pretty good job with the place. After his death, well, a farm goes downhill fast."

"Yeah," she agreed. "Weeds'll choke a garden in a matter of days." She let out a long sigh. "There's more work than I'd planned on. Hadn't planned on any, really."

"Yes, I know. The worst of it'll be fixing the kitchen. Your chicken coop, though, if it were me, I'd have a new one built. The fence could wait if—"

"Speaking of the fence, I was considering the hay. I think I'll run a small herd. If Leroy was doing it, it must be worth the effort."

"Oh, is money...?" He trailed off, realizing he'd overstepped.

"I ain't broke. Jeremiah left me some funds, but they won't last forever. This place will need to pay its way."

The screen door banged behind them and Ruth stepped outside, carrying a tray of lemonade. She set it down on the porch. "Noemie, if you'll pour, I'm going to bring a few chairs out here for us."

In short order, Ruth had rounded up three chairs and a low walnut coffee table for the porch. Mismatched and formal for outside furniture, but at least the chairs were comfortable, and Montgomery was glad for the seat. Much better than sitting on pine steps. He and Noemie settled across from each other and sipped on their lemonade, cold from the spring.

"If you want to turn this place into a profitable farm again, Noemie, I reckon you should plant some corn and tobacco. The value is high right now because of the war."

"Good crops."

"Your acreage down by the river will grow corn fifteen feet tall or I'm not a Boaze."

Ruth sat down with them, presenting another tray

loaded with biscuits and slices of ham, cheese, and apples. "Oh, this looks good." Noemie's stomach growled. As she reached for a biscuit, Ruth quickly offered a prayer, slowing Noemie's hand, but Montgomery noted she didn't stop completely to observe the moment. He remembered a time when Noemie had been noted for her long-winded prayers over the family food. He decided not to question her about it.

"Ruth, Montgomery is suggesting we put in some cash crops. Corn and tobacco. What's your farming background?"

"If we can plant it, I can tend it."

Noemie nodded, chewed on her bottom lip for a moment. "Putting this place back together is going to take a big pinch out of my money. I want you in on the decision."

Ruth smiled, a lovely, warm expression that showed her affection for her mother-in-law, and it moved Montgomery. If only he were a younger man...

"This is yer home place. I heard ye say it must pay for itself. It's good land. We've got two strong backs. It'll work."

"You won't do it alone," Montgomery said firmly, scratching his bearded jaw. "I can help, and I will. We're family." He winked at Noemie. "If you'll claim me."

A smile lit the woman's face, a smile that seemed a little mischievous to Montgomery, but sweet. "Be careful what you wish for."

———

A BLACK SNAKE in the kitchen that evening prompted Noemie and Ruth to agree on clearing the weeds away from the house and the yard first. Ruth insisted she would take on this chore and Noemie could get the inside of her house in order. Everything except for the kitchen. The carpenters would have to do their part first.

Ruth spent two days cutting away and burning briars, dog fennel, and bull thistles, along with tons of ivy and honeysuckle.

She hated cutting down the honeysuckle, its fragrance and blossoms were so beautiful. Noemie assured her, however, that there was plenty growing along the fence near the barn.

Soon, the foundations of the house were clear of critter-hiding vines, a yard appeared from the wild chaos of weeds, and a stone path re-emerged from the dirt. The area where the kitchen garden once lived was the next chore. They weeded and hoed up a hundred-foot square plot and planned its contents.

They hung a quilt over the broken kitchen window at night, knowing full well it only gave a false sense of security. Neither woman, however, could stand the thought of the window open to the outside world. They hoped the blanket would at least stop critters such as squirrels and snakes. A mischievous man, on the other hand, wouldn't be stopped at all.

The third evening after a particularly hot, exhaustive day, they sat on the porch enjoying the cool twilight, trying to find the strength to cook some supper. "I swear, I'm done in," Noemie said. "Didn't work as hard today, but the heat." She shook her head. "Don't like it much anymore."

Ruth agreed. "Sucks the life out of me. I've no energy at all. I miss our evenings of chatting and knitting. Now, it's all I can do to keep my eyes open."

"It won't be like this forever." Noemie scanned the yard

with a pleased expression. "We'll get caught up. We've already done more than I thought we would."

They sat in silence another few minutes, Ruth's mind running along a dozen different tracks. Strange how they all seemed to intersect with Mr. Boaze. He made her wonder if she would marry again. Noemie had said when the war was over, men would be coming home. She wondered if there was someone else out there for her. On a whim, she asked, "Tell me about yer first husband, Noemie."

The woman smiled, almost a little sadly. "He was my first love. We met at a barn dance. Oh, Lord, I was smitten, but it took months for us to get together."

"What was the delay?"

"Luke was twenty-four. I was fifteen and a bit of a flibbertigibbet. He said he wanted to make sure I knew what I wanted."

"Oh, sounds as if he was quite sure of himself."

Noemie chuckled. "And he knew there's nothing like wanting something you can't have. He must have dangled that bone in front of me six months or more."

"I don't understand. What did he do?"

"We had one dance, and he said that did it for him, but he had to be sure of me. So, he talked to me at parties and such, but he wouldn't hang about or ask me to dance. If he ran into me in town, he would chat and then walk away without asking to call on me or even inviting me for a walk, but I *knew* he wanted to. I could see it in his eyes." She fell quiet for a long, thoughtful spell, then finally said, "He kept himself just out of my reach. Drove me crazy. All the other boys fell away. I didn't want anybody but Luke. I couldn't see being with anybody but Luke."

Ruth was enthralled. "And? How did ye finally get together?"

"One night at a wedding reception, he walked up to me and asked, 'You done yet?' Well, I knew what he meant. And I said yes, and he kissed me. We were married a month later."

"Were you happy with him?"

"Very." Her brow pinched. "His death liked to have killed me. If it hadn't been for James, I don't know if I'd have been able to get out of bed." Noemie reached out and laid her hand on Ruth's. "I know it hurts now, Ruth, and you think you can't love again. James would want you to be happy. Don't feel guilty when the healing starts. And it will."

Guilt twisted in the pit of Ruth's stomach. It broke her heart how little she mourned James, because such slight grief would hurt the one person she did truly, deeply love: his mother. She squeezed Noemie's hand and said, "I will remember."

Noemie stood and stretched, rolling her shoulders. "I swanny, I sleep like a log in that bed. How about you? You sleeping all right or wandering the house looking for intruders?"

Ruth sighed and stood as well. "I go to bed thinking I'll stay awake and listen for a bit. The next thing I know, it's morning."

"Well, ain't neither one of us a Nervous Nelly."

"I think… " How could she say this in a way Noemie would receive? "The Lord has His angels watching over us. If we need to wake, I think we will. At least, I'll trust in Him and not worry."

"Well, trust in Him for the both of us." She patted Ruth on the shoulder and went inside.

Ruth released a sad, weary sigh and followed her in.

CHAPTER SIX

MONTGOMERY AND HIS YOUNG FARMHAND, BEAR, DROVE UP to the house just as Noemie and Ruth were coming down the front steps. He tipped his hat and eyed the freshly cleared yard with a satisfied nod. "Looks a thousand percent better already."

"We're getting there an inch at a time," Noemie said, watching Bear jump down from the wagon. She recognized him from town. He was a tall, thick, blonde-haired German boy with eyes as blue as a deep fjord. He was also built like a grizzly.

Montgomery set the brake and jumped down from the wagon as well. "Ladies, this is Bjorn—"

"Thought you said his name was Bear," Noemie interrupted.

"Yah," the boy extended his meaty hand in greeting and the two shook. "My name means Bear in German."

"What do you want us to call you?"

"Bear is good. The hands at Mr. Boaze's told me it means I am strong and big like a bear."

Montgomery kicked at a stone, a little embarrassed. "Started out as kind of a joke, but now that they've all gotten to know Bear, there's real respect behind the name."

Ruth offered her hand. "I'm Ruth."

"My daughter-in-law," Noemie volunteered.

"It is good to meet you."

"So, you ladies on your way out?"

"We're picking up some seeds for the kitchen garden. A few other things. Didn't know you were coming by."

"I meant to come sooner, but I needed to get Bear here cleared up of some projects. Today, he and I are going to get that tree off your roof." He considered the project for a moment, then slid his gaze to Noemie. "Why don't I measure the window? You could order a replacement while you're in town. The sooner the better, if you want it here before fall."

"Good idea. What about the rest of the work?"

"One of my hands is a fine carpenter and he's coming tomorrow. He and Bear should get your kitchen fixed up pretty quick."

"Mighty kind of you to help us out, Montgomery. Lord knows there's enough work here to keep an army of hands hopping." Noemie gently shouldered Ruth toward him. "You get the measurements. Write 'em down. I'll get the wagon hitched up." She turned and strode toward the barn.

Ruth scrambled after Montgomery and Bear, scrounging for a piece of paper from her reticule. Montgomery unfolded his ruler and he and Bear measured the window. When Ruth could not produce a pencil, he gave her the one from behind his ear with a smile. Their fingers touched as he passed it to her. Again, he tried not to misread anything, but he would have sworn her gaze lingered a breath of a second longer than necessary.

"We won't be gone long, Montgomery," Noemie yelled, driving the wagon from the barn. "You need anything from town?"

Ruth curtsied and rushed to catch her waiting ride.

Montgomery watched the girl climb up beside her mother-in-law. Did he need anything? For the longest time, he'd thought no. But now, something stretched and yawned in him, coming to life. He shook his head, a little puzzled by his strange thoughts. "No, thank you, though. We'll most likely be here when you get back." He snapped his fingers. "Actually..." He handed the folding ruler to Bear and jogged down to the wagon. "Listen, Noemie, you see Sheriff Holden in town, you should be extra nice to him."

Not surprisingly, his cousin scowled. "Why? Reese mad at me for some reason?"

"Well, uh," Montgomery tugged on his ear, then decided to spit it out. "He was going to come out and charge you with disrupting the peace in the café. And threatening Leroy. Leroy wanted to press charges. I talked him out of it. Witlow didn't want to bother, either. He said you were going to pay for the damages. If you're going to the café —"

"I don't need to be reminded of my word, Montgomery Boaze. I said I'd pay. Witlow knows my word is good. Leroy can go suck an egg." Noemie snapped the reins and drove the wagon on down the driveway. Ruth glanced back and gave him a what-are-we-going-to-do-with-her shrug.

He nodded in return and continued to watch them for a minute, pushing away an unexpected restlessness in his spirit. Bear strode up beside him with a questioning gaze, snapping Montgomery out of his reverie. He playfully tagged Bear in the gut. "Let's get those tools out of the wagon and jump on this. We're burning daylight."

———

HEYWARD'S MOUTH watered over the full plate of fried chicken legs and potato salad his maid set in front of him. "That's all, Bessie." He excused the black woman with an arrogance that came from the world he'd built around him. A world he liked and meant to keep.

He took a bite and ruminated on his wealth. He was quite proud of himself for purchasing a home in town, on the main thoroughfare into Walhalla. A pretty, clapboard-sided Gothic Revival home, it announced his money to everyone coming into Walhalla. He moved in the right circles now, too. He was at the mayor's regularly, making donations. He owned several small businesses and had purchased half a dozen farms throughout the county. A few maybe he hadn't gotten by the most legal means, but there was no one around to argue with him—

His cousin's face leaped before his eyes as if to dispute the point and he threw the chicken leg back down on his plate.

Noemie had come back and tied one big knot into his plans. Cost him time, money, and one of the biggest farms of his holdings.

And if he sat back and did nothing to get the farm back, ol' Boaze was likely to wander in and sweet- talk his cousin right out of her land. He was already acting like their holy savior, pushing Leroy not to press charges against the woman. Of course, in the end, that was best. He should draw as little attention as possible to this knot. Till he got things figured out. The woman just drove him to distraction.

He picked up a salad fork and bent it slowly, without thought, between his fingers as a sneer curled his lip.

He had to get the farm from Noemie somehow and make sure she didn't learn of the fake deed. Once she saw a forged signature, there would be all kinds of hell to pay. And Leroy Heyward would not be buying any farms from jail.

For now, she had to believe he'd lied to everybody about buying the property. A rich man trying to look richer.

But what now? If she would just sell to him, quietly, privately...

He had nosed around the property the other night just to see if they had a hired hand or what improvements they'd made, and the Irish girl had almost caught him. That would have looked bad, and it had been a foolish idea. He needed to be smarter about this. Stop these mistakes.

He laid his hands on each side of his plate and drummed his fingers. "What to do, what to do with you, cousin. I need your land."

The honey pot on the table next to the still-warm biscuits was an answer of sorts. "Yeah, I reckon I can always try the sweet approach first."

If she played along, life would be pleasant, easy, uncomplicated.

'Cause he sure hated to take the hard road with his cousin.

Yeah, he hated to resort—

A buggy passing by happened to catch his eye. Like a

schoolboy trying to steal a glimpse of his crush, he went to the dining room window and peered out.

Well, if it isn't Darla, Miss La-ti-da herself. Running errands for Lord Boaze. And looking pretty as a picture.

Hayward glanced back at his meal. He should stay and eat. Turn away from Darla's inexplicable hold on him, this maddening chaos of love and hate roiling in his chest.

But the pull was too strong.

A few minutes later, he found Darla's wagon parked in front of the feed store. He hemmed and hawed for a minute, nodded at a few passers-by, and decided to wait for her. He went around to the side of the building and stood where he could just see the boardwalk and her wagon.

In the high-noon sun beating down on him, his temple throbbed. He touched the dent there and scowled at the memory. A thirteen-year-old girl in pigtails who couldn't stand the attention from a boy so in love he didn't know which end was up. He'd merely offered her a smile—

No, that wasn't honest. He'd done more than smile. He'd grabbed hold of her, tried to stop her from running. He'd only wanted her to listen, listen to how much he loved her. That he couldn't sleep at night for thinking of her.

Darla had responded with a rock to his forehead.

The old wound pulsed. In his mind, Leroy had always thought her reaction had been overly aggressive. He'd been a little forceful with her, but there had been no call for—

The bell over the feed store jangled and Darla crossed Leroy's field of vision. As she was placing a box in the back of the wagon, he sidled up beside her. A quick glance at the street showed only light traffic and folks engrossed in their own business.

"Afternoon, Darla."

She gasped and stepped back, her hand at her throat. "Leroy. What are you doing here?"

He tried to ignore the disdain in her eyes, the tension in her body. She had her pretty auburn hair pulled back and twisted into a bun. "I like the braid you normally wear better." The observation sounded out of place and he offered a placating smile. "Just happened to be passing by. Wanted to say hello."

She inched back. He inched forward. He liked this game.

"I told you to please quit bothering me." Her entrancing jade eyes sparkled with fear.

She was jittery, nervous. He rattled her. Emboldened, he attempted to touch her cheek and she swatted his hand away. Anger flared in his chest, but he tamped it down. "I see you on the street, I have a right to say hello."

"But not to touch me," she fired back. Her tone drew glances from townsfolk, and she lowered her voice. "Leave me alone, or I'll get another rock."

Automatically, he touched his temple. He remembered well. Her glaring down at him, her freckled face smeared with dirt and tears, her mouth twisted up in a sneer. Then the blinding explosion of pain in his skull.

The worms in his brain squirmed faster, the memory of the pain bright and fresh.

He cocked his head a little as a thought occurred to him. "You're not twice my size anymore." Like a kid measuring who's taller, he laid his hand atop her head and slid it across the air between them to touch his chest.

"Why, you don't even hardly come up to my breastbone." He lowered his voice. "Maybe next time *I'll* use the rock."

Darla inhaled sharply, froze for a moment, then shook her head. "I'm not afraid of you." She pushed him away. "I'm not afraid of you," she repeated, climbing up into the wagon.

Leroy didn't say anything else. He stepped back and let her go, but the further away she drove, the bigger his grin grew.

CHAPTER SEVEN

For the week that Montgomery, Bear, and the carpenters worked on the kitchen, Noemie and Ruth worked on the vegetable garden. Finally, on Friday evening, as the shadows fell across the newly hoed rows, Noemie planted the last of the corn kernels.

She straightened up and arched her back. Pain like little fireflies flitted up and down her spine. "I'll be, this is harder than I remember."

Ruth rose from her knees where she'd been nailing the fence slats back in place. "Aye, it's the hardest I've worked since I left Ireland." She dropped the hammer in a toolbox and stepped back to survey the fence. "It needs painting, but at least now it will keep the rabbits out."

"That's a start."

The screen door slammed, and they looked up at the sound. A moment later, Montgomery came around the corner of the house. "Thought y'all were inside."

"Nope." Noemie held back a smile as he surveyed the

garden on his approach and tried not to look like he was also looking at Ruth.

"Everything planted?" he asked.

"Believe so," Ruth said.

He rested his hand on the fence and nodded approval. "We've patched the roof, replaced all the wet wood in the kitchen, and framed in a window opening. You get the replacement ordered, Noemie?"

"I did. Won't be here until July."

Montgomery frowned, took his hat off, and ran his fingers through his sweaty, shaggy hair. "Well, would you like us to hang a quilt over it or board it up while you wait?"

Noemie and Ruth looked at each other. Ruth scrunched up her face. "It makes the kitchen impossibly dark. We hang a quilt up at night."

"Yeah," Noemie agreed. But she didn't like leaving it open to the elements, either. She snapped her fingers over an idea. "Montgomery, what about the wagon tarp?"

He shrugged. "Should work. White canvas will let in light but keep out the bugs."

"I'll get it from the barn," Ruth offered, leaving the enclosed garden with her toolbox in hand. She paused to swing the gate closed, opened it, closed it again. It swung smoothly and latched as it should.

Noemie chuckled at her. "You did a fine job on the fence and the gate. Thank you, Ruth."

The girl beamed with satisfaction. "We're right capable, ye and I."

She strode off toward the barn, grinning at Montgomery as she skirted past him. Noemie watched him watching Ruth. The gleam in his eyes made her heart ache for James. Her son, who would never fall in love now, or bounce babies on his knee. Never kiss Noemie on the cheek and wish her a happy birthday. So many nevers. But she loved Ruth as much as she would a daughter, and she could be pragmatic about the girl's future. "I almost didn't bring her with me. I tried to make her go back to her people in Ireland."

"I'm glad she didn't. I mean, I bet you're glad you didn't. Make her leave."

"She's been more help than I can say." Noemie brushed her hands together, shedding the last of the dirt. "Now, I want to talk to you about the corn and tobacco idea. And I think I am gonna get some cattle from ya, if you're still of a mind to sell me some."

"Of course."

"I'd invite ya to supper so we could talk about it, get down to brass tacks, but honestly, son, I'm beat, and I won't presume Ruth has the energy to cook a meal."

"Why don't you two come over to my place for supper? I've got a housekeeper. Darla. She said this morning she was making chicken and dumplings."

Noemie wasn't sure she could drag herself to the basin, but the promise of chicken and dumplings made her mouth water. She and Ruth hadn't had anything but cold suppers for over a week, and she was getting mighty tired of crackers, cheese, and canned peaches. "You sure it wouldn't be an inconvenience to her?"

"She always makes plenty."

———

RUTH SUCKED in a breath as the wagon rounded a curve and Montgomery's house and fields came into view. The scene was as picturesque as a painting. The sky above the prim, white farmhouse glowed with the warm hues of a setting sun, but the vivid reds and oranges were giving way quickly to the night. The silhouettes of distant mountains rose up behind his land like guardians. The hills surrounding the house were all either green and thick with milling cattle or tilled and pungent, the freshly planted fields waiting on the crops to spring forth.

"My," Ruth breathed. "He's done quite well for himself. A regular lord, he is."

"I always knew he'd do well." Noemie urged the horse on for a little more speed. "Went through a rough patch when he was young, but he grew out of it. He had a fine reputation when we left ten years ago. He's generous and honest."

Ruth smiled tenderly at Noemie, noting the little, painful dip in her brow. "As was James," she said as a comfort. And he had been both those things. His only flaw had been his devotion to work, thinking his wife would be fine untended.

Noemie's lips tightened and she wiggled her nose to stop a sniffle, but Ruth saw the gleam of appreciation in her eyes, the hint of tears. She patted her mother-in-law on the thigh and let the silence lie.

———

MONTGOMERY MUST HAVE HEARD their wagon. As they pulled up, he strode from the house, a pipe in one hand, spectacles in the other, as if they'd interrupted his evening reading. A man came from the barn and held the horse by its halter.

"Noemie, Ruth, glad you could make it. Supper's ready."

He looked at the man. "Billy, why don't you feed and water their mare?"

"Will do."

Montgomery led them through a home Ruth would have described as modest, humble, comfortable. A place that immediately made her feel welcome with its warm, unpretentious furnishings. Like the man. Montgomery was easy to be around. She understood why Noemie thought so highly of him.

He seated each of them at a long table, and a moment later, the housekeeper poked her head in from the kitchen. "Everyone here?" She was an older woman, closer in age to Noemie, but pretty in the elegant way the years affect some. Auburn hair twisted on her head reflected the candlelight, and wide, green eyes danced with delight, especially when they landed on Noemie. "Glory be. He said you were back, Noemie."

"Darla? Darla *May?*" Noemie emphasized the last word.

"None other." Darla slipped over to Noemie, who stood, and the two hugged like long- lost friends. Or cousins?

"Tell me," Ruth asked, "is she a cousin, too?"

Noemie chuckled and sat back down. "No, Miss Sassy Pants. We were best friends from when we were, what, ten?"

"Eleven," Darla corrected, resting a hand on Noemie's shoulder. "A lot of water under the bridge since then, huh?"

"About an ocean's worth, I reckon. You moved right after I got married. To Atlanta, wasn't it?"

"Yep. I've only been back in Oconee County for a few months." She shivered, as if something gave her a chill. "Leroy Heyward didn't move away, unfortunately. He's just as disturbing as ever."

"He still carrying a torch for you?"

Darla flicked an uneasy glance at Montgomery. "He's been downright frightening, following me in town, accosting me on the sidewalk and such."

"I remember one time you walloped him upside the head for getting fresh with ya."

"He was half my size then."

Montgomery's expression darkened, his brow tensed, a warning like the clouds before a storm. "I had a few harsh words with him at the mayor's the other night. I thought I'd set him straight."

The housekeeper exhaled but Ruth didn't think she heard much relief in it.

"I'm sorry you got dragged into anything, Montgomery, but thank you."

He shrugged as if it was nothing to protect a woman. The conversation sagged then, heavy with awkwardness.

"Well..." Noemie nodded. "It's good to see you, Darla. You'll have to come by the farm and we'll do some catching up."

"I will, for sure. Right now, let me get dinner out to you folks. Montgomery isn't paying me to jabber." Darla slipped back into the kitchen with a wink, but Ruth thought the lightheartedness was a little forced.

"My, my, my," Noemie muttered. "Seems a thousand years since I was a girl running barefoot through these hills...but it feels like it was yesterday, too."

"Time sure is flying by," Montgomery agreed. "One day Bryl is playing on a swing in the backyard. The next, he's carrying a rifle at West Point."

Noemie flinched. "What are they doing with those boys?"

"Some have enlisted, but the government hasn't called

the school up yet. Bryl's still there. I got a letter today. He said West Point is taking the class of '64 and moving their graduation to '63."

"Hmm." Noemie picked up a fork and fidgeted with it.

"Maybe the war will be over before then," Ruth offered with sincere hope.

Darla entered with a steaming pot of chicken and dumplings, the mouthwatering aroma filling the room. "I'm with Montgomery on this," she said, beginning to ladle out the chicken. Won't be a ten-year war, but it's going to be long."

The conversation remained subdued after that, none of them willing or able to get past their worries. Montgomery directed the talk of crops and cattle and when and how to get things started, but their minds all seemed to be elsewhere.

When they finished, he moved them to the porch and Darla served coffee by candlelight. Ruth sat on the rail, her back resting against a post, sipping her drink and gazing out at the moon rising over the ridge. Stars flickered and blinked on the grand stage, crickets sang, and a lonely owl called for his mate. The mountains in the distance whispered to her, begged her to come exploring.

"It's so beautiful here," she said to no one in particular. "How could ye have left it, Noemie?"

"I love my foothills and mountains, but I loved Jeremiah more. And James needed a father." She took a thoughtful sip of coffee and sighed. "But it sure feels good to be back."

"Before Bryl's involvement, I believed I could ignore the war. That was naive on my part. Between refugees and deserters, the war is hitting here one way or the other. It's not a refuge anymore."

"Do ye not own any slaves, Mr. Boaze?" It occurred to

Ruth she hadn't seen any about the place. The man who took care of the horse was white.

"Ruth, I wish you'd call me Montgomery. Everyone does."

She bobbed her head in acquiescence. "Montgomery." She liked the sound of his name on her lips.

"And, no. I don't cotton to it. Never have."

"This valley was built by hard-working pioneer stock," Noemie said proudly. "We do it ourselves or *hire* help. Nobody owns anybody here."

"You might find it interesting to know," Montgomery began, "your cousin has departed from that ideology. He is the largest slaveholder in the Upstate. When he's not beating them, he's working over two hundred souls on farms around here."

Noemie sneered in disgust. "He is a disappointment to humanity, to put it politely."

Ruth found the juxtaposition of hired labor vs. slave labor fascinating...and Montgomery's success well-deserved. "Ironic, yer holdings are more successful. And I'm glad of it."

"God is good. I would never buy and sell another human. I treat my hired hands fairly and pay a fair wage."

Noemie patted his hand. "You always were a decent, honest man, Montgomery. You can't buy that kind of a reputation. Your farm prospers because of your integrity."

Montgomery squirmed, as if he were uncomfortable with the compliments, and changed the subject away from himself. "And we'll get your farm up and running quick," he said. "We've got a plan in place. Things will move right along, assuming the weather cooperates this summer."

"When has it ever done that?" Noemie asked with a bitter tone.

"We can't be looking for the darkness, Noemie," Ruth cautioned. "It'll be too easy to find. Let's keep our eyes on the Light. We'll get our crops planted, the fence repaired, the cattle delivered, and we'll trust in the Lord to take care of us."

Noemie sniffed with what sounded like disdain but didn't say anything. Ruth knew she wanted to air her grievances with God once again, but the woman held back.

"She's right, Noemie. All we can do is our best. Then we pray and leave it in God's hands." Montgomery reached for his coffee. "Tomorrow, Bear'll fix the fence Heyward tore down, then I'll get him started on plowing. Caleb and his brother should have you a new chicken coop lickety split. Come back tomorrow and we'll cut you out some cattle. Your farm will be paying its way in no time."

Noemie raised her coffee cup. "Then here's to the homestead on Frying Pan Ridge."

Montgomery met her cup with his. "Frying Pan Ridge."

Ruth joined them, adding, "May the Lord bless it, and make His face to shine upon it."

———

"Jumpin' Jehoshaphat, look at him go." Noemie hugged the bag of corn kernels to her breast and marveled at Bear's strength and skill behind the plow. The draft horse, Penelope, sensed his confidence, and together they cut through the unbroken ground as if it were no denser than mud. Shaking her head, she cut her eyes at Ruth. "You ready?"

Ruth raised up the seeder by its opposing handles. "Fill the hold."

Noemie poured seed into the tank, and Ruth began

walking, stopping to deposit seeds every twelve inches or so. Noemie trailed behind, covering the kernels in dirt with her toe, refilling Ruth's tank as necessary. By noon, they had planted a third of the field and Bear had plowed almost two-thirds of it. When they stopped for lunch in the shade by the bustling creek, she was tickled with the progress.

"Bear, your momma didn't raise a shirker." Noemie handed him a boiled egg and some cheese. "I've never seen anybody plow with that speed."

"Thank you, ma'am. I like plowing. Gives me time to think."

"And what is it ye think about?" Ruth settled down and leaned back on a tall pine, appreciating the scent of it, mixing with the cool air rising up from the water. She took a bite of her egg and smiled knowingly at the boy.

Bear's cheeks, flushed from his work, brightened even more. "Ah, just...things."

"I'd say by the color spreading over yer face, these *things* must be pretty, petite, with blue eyes?"

The boy blushed impossibly red and Noemie guffawed. "Land sakes, you're gonna give the boy a stroke, Ruth."

"Oh, Bear, I'm sorry. I didn't mean to embarrass ye. I was just having a bit of fun."

The boy hung his head, stared hard at the egg in his hand, and sighed loudly. "She's sixteen, with *red* hair, a patch of freckles across her nose..." He looked up. "And, yah, eyes the color of the sky on a September morn. And she don't know I'm alive."

Ruth *tsked*. "Oh, what a foolish, foolish girl."

"What's the matter with her? She need glasses or something?" Noemie asked in her abrupt way.

Bear laughed and the tension over his heartbreak eased. "Maybe if I could work up the gumption to talk to her—"

"You ain't talked to her?"

"No, ma'am."

"What are you waiting on?" Noemie knew she was being abrupt but thought maybe a little directness might help the boy.

"She's just so pretty and—"

"And you're one handsome rascal. You need to do the girl a favor and speak to her. Tell her that her eyes turn your knees to water. That'll do it."

Bear's eyes had widened to the size of quarters. "I couldn't say that. I—"

"You can say it. You say it with your head up and your shoulders squared. Say it like it's the most truthful thing you're ever gonna let pass your lips."

The boy gulped. "What—what if I did say it? Then what?"

"Long as she ain't otherwise attached, I'd say she'll be inclined to hear a little more."

"More?"

It had been so long since Noemie had given love advice that she'd forgotten how much she'd enjoyed sharing her wisdom with James and his friends. And this boy reminded her a little of James. "A woman likes confidence, Bear. It's a hard thing to resist. It don't mean you're stuck-up or prideful. Just that you're honest and have good intentions toward things, including her." She closed one eye and studied him. "You do have honorable intentions, don't you?"

"Oh, yah, yes, ma'am."

"Fine, then. While you're out there finishing this field, you think of some more nice things to say. But remember, you don't go up to her with your head down, staring at the ground, kicking stones. No, sir. You look that little girl right in the eye. You say something real complimentary and straight forward. And then you know what you do?"

The boy was leaning forward as if Noemie was sharing the secret of the universe. "No, what?"

"You walk away."

"What?"

"You walk away. Don't be rude. Say your piece and then move on, like you've got things to do and so does she."

"I don't know…"

"Bear, you've got one chance to give that little girl something to think about you. Will it be how strong, handsome, and bold you are? Or, you're a daisy with legs?"

"Well, I don't think I want to be a daisy…" He thought for a moment, popped the last bite of egg into his mouth, and climbed to his feet. "I will ponder things, Miss Noemie."

When he was out of earshot, Noemie looked over at Ruth, who was wearing a wistful grin as she plucked peta l s from a flower. "What are you grinning at?"

"The first time I met James, he strode up to my desk, looked me in the eye, and said, 'Miss Ruth, your laugh is so pretty and musical, it makes me want to pick roses for ye.' Well, as you can imagine, he left me speechless." She narrowed her eyes at Noemie. "And then he walked away." Ruth raised one accusatory eyebrow at Noemie.

CHAPTER EIGHT

HEYWARD SURE HAD MEANT TO GET OUT TO NOEMIE'S LONG before now, but a constant parade of problems at this farm or that business had kept him tied up. The life of an entrepreneur.

He scowled as he dismounted in the yard and looked around. They'd improved the place right much. The yard had been cleared and tidied. Weeds around the barn and house had been removed. He glanced over at the window where a tarp covered the opening. It was nailed to new wood. The roof had been repaired, as well.

Not liking how settled things looked, he wrapped his horse's reins around the hitching post. Two women couldn't do this work on their own. The place reeked of Montgomery Boaze's good deeds.

Well, he wasn't the only one in the county who could help out a couple of widows. Leroy stomped up to the front door and pounded on it. After a moment of silence, he hammered again and called out. "Noemie. It's me, Leroy. You about?"

Still nothing.

He contemplated letting himself in and snooping, but thought better of it. Good thing. A second later, he heard approaching voices. Heyward strode to the end of the porch overlooking most of the farm and caught sight of Noemie, Ruth, and some blond man striding out from behind the barn, a saddled mare following them. Heyward waved and hurried down to greet them.

"Noemie, Miss Ruth," he tipped his hat, while taking in the sight of their dirty faces, hands black with soil, dresses smudged top to bottom with dirt. Beside them, the fella turned out to be a mere boy. "Don't I know you?"

"Probably seen me around," he said with no hint of malice.

"This is Bear. He's helping out. You'd best get on back, son. We'll see ya in the morning and finish that field by the oak grove."

"Yes, ma'am." He immediately swung up into the saddle, nodded a goodbye, and took off at a trot.

Before he'd gone a dozen feet, Noemie turned on Heyward. "What are you doing here? Come to try to take something else from me?"

While he had not expected her to be nice, he'd thought maybe she'd be civil. Still, he was committed. At least for this stage of the game. "Now, Noemie, I reckon we could try to let bygones be bygones. You've got your farm back, and you look like you're doing well." He glanced around again. "Real well."

Noemie waved him off dismissively and started walking toward the house, Ruth in tow. "No thanks to you. I appreciate you moving your cattle, but you could have left the fence intact."

Heyward hurried along behind them. "That was unintentional, and I really meant to send a man out here to fix it."

"Good intentions don't do the dishes. Besides, I'll not have slaves on my property. You're a disappointment, Leroy, through and through." Noemie stomped up the stairs but paused in the middle of the porch. She looked over her shoulder at Heyward, who tried to don a peevish grin. "I'm gonna sit down and have a sip of water before I do anything else. You're welcome to sit a spell, Leroy, but don't overstay it."

The women disappeared into the house, leaving him at a loss at her cold invitation. Her ingrained Christian hospitality, he supposed. He could hear them in the kitchen and wandered over to the tarp. A pump handle squeaked, metal clinked, and a moment later, the sound of water, splashing and gurgling, came to him.

"We'll be right out, Leroy. Sit down," she commanded. "You want some water?"

"Uh, yes, please," he said, trying to sound contrite.

When the women joined him, they had washed the dirt off their hands and faces and were carrying tin mugs of ice-cold water. He took a sip and nodded with sincere appreciation. The spring on Noemie's property was a good one. "You've done a lot of work around here."

"Some," she said flatly.

"You got a lot more to do." He noticed the Irish girl didn't say much, but she was a watcher. "Got ya a good lookin' chicken coop now. I see you put a new fence around the hog pen. Who did all the work for ya?" He suspected he knew the answer but asked anyway.

"Montgomery sent a couple of fellas over."

Montgomery. He let his gaze skip past the ladies to a

freshly plowed field. "You putting in crops? That's gonna keep you busy."

"I think we can keep the work from cutting into our heavy social schedule," she said. "Only one ball a month."

Leroy winced at her sarcasm but didn't respond. He kept picturing the honey jar on his dining room table. "I thought maybe we could talk about me leasing some land from you. I'd still like to run cattle. You've got rich, pretty fields."

"Yes, I do. And we're gonna put our own cattle on them. I'm buying some from Montgomery."

He held his face still, intent on not betraying his dissatisfaction with the news. "You got a lot of land. You still might could lease me a hundred acres or so. How big a herd you gonna have?"

"Maybe a couple hundred head, but we're planting corn and tobacco, too."

"That's a lot of work for two women, Noemie, and just one field hand."

"You said that." She narrowed her eyes at him. "What do you really want, Leroy?"

He finished off his water and set the cup down. "I came to make you an offer on the place. The whole spread. Cash on the barrel head."

"I'm right annoyed with you, Leroy. The way you just thought you'd waltz in here and take it didn't sit well with me. Not at all. You're lucky I let you on the porch, much less gave you something to drink."

He shook his head and tried to look ashamed. "It was just sitting here, falling into ruin, cousin. I didn't think you'd ever come back, especially when Cyrus passed, and nobody came asking after him or this place."

"The war. I thought it was interfering with the mail."

She slammed her cup down. "Don't matter anyhow. You were fixing to steal my place and you lied about a deed. Why'd you do that?"

He swallowed a big piece of humble pie. "I was trying to build myself up, Noemie. Look and sound important. People think you got money, it opens doors." *It opens more when you can produce a deed...* " I was trying to build up my—"

"Your bank account."

"Reputation, I was gonna say. There's nothing wrong with building up a bank account, either. I didn't steal your farm, and I gave it back when you asked for it."

She frowned. "Yeah, you did." The woman softened a little. "You didn't have a leg to stand on, but you did get off the property quick."

"I don't want there to be hard feelings between us, cousin. And I would sincerely like to buy the place if you're selling. You and your little daughter-in-law there should have a smaller place, something more manageable." Leroy stopped, instantly realizing his mistake.

Noemie's spine straightened, her chin came up, and a flinty edge glimmered in her cold, catlike eyes. "We'll do just fine. We may be women, but we're not invalids. I'm not selling. Not to you. Not to anybody."

"All right." He sighed. "All right. I'll quit asking then."

Because the time for talking was over. He stood and swiped his hat off the back of his chair. "Still, you need anything, give a yell. Oh, and be watchful. A bear's been spotted in the valley."

———

RUTH HAD A SENSE ABOUT PEOPLE. Especially if she could simply listen and watch, not engage with them. Leroy Heyward did not like being watched, she figured that much. He was a bit fidgety, as if much of what came out of his mouth was a lie he'd need to remember later. But there was something else, something dark and malevolent behind his eyes, like a wolf waiting in the shadows. She kept all this to herself, though, as she and Noemie watched him ride off the farm.

"Don't think much of him, do ya?"

"I think he doesn't say what he means."

"And what's that mean?"

Ruth shrugged, unable to explain the feeling. "It's as if he says one thing, but the look in his eyes says he's thinking something different. Something...hateful."

"I suspect he's peeved about not getting this farm, but he'll get over it."

Ruth supposed that could be true. "What if he doesn't? Ye think he'll cause us trouble?"

Noemie gave it hard consideration, judging by the intense expression on her face. "I don't know. I've been gone a long time. He seems more ambitious than I recall, but that don't make him dangerous."

Ruth couldn't say one way or the other, not for certain. "I hope not."

———

THE NEXT DAY, a livestock wagon pulled into the yard. Ruth and Noemie had seen it from the field and walked up to investigate. The high, wooden sides caged a restless, snorting hog in back.

"What ya got there?" Noemie asked, eyeing the pink-and-black spotted animal moving about.

"Compliments of Mr. Heyward. He said ya need a hog for your hog pen."

Noemie continued her survey of the animal. "Well, uh, can we pay ya for it or—?"

"No, ma'am. She's absolutely a gift. I was to make that clear to ya."

"Well..." Noemie trailed off.

Ruth stepped up beside her. "Do ye think he's attached strings to the gift?"

"Could be a peace offering." Noemie set her jaw and looked at the driver. "Tell him thank you for us. Makes up for the fence he took out when he moved his cattle."

A little while later, Ruth and Noemie watched their new hog rooting around and snorting happily in the pen. "She's a beast," Ruth said. "I've seen few hogs bigger."

"Yep. A good six- maybe eight-hundred pounds. She had to cost Leroy a pretty penny."

"And ye sure there's no strings attached?"

"I don't care if there are. Far as I'm concerned, Priscilla there just makes us even."

CHAPTER NINE

RUTH RUBBED HER NECK WITH DIRT-STAINED HANDS AND SAT down on the porch steps. "Praise God, everything is planted. Now we pray for rain."

Noemie dropped beside her and sighed. "Our luck, He'll send a drought—"

"Noemie," Ruth cut her off. "Ye must stop speaking curses over us. I love ye to death, ye know that. But Scripture says life and death is in the power of the tongue. Don't speak forth any trouble upon us."

Noemie frowned, clearly annoyed, but suddenly she drooped and nodded. "I admire that you've kept your mind on things above, girl. You have an admirable outlook on life. I'll just hold my tongue."

"I'm sorry. I don't mean to scold—"

"No, it's all right. I'll save my comments for the middle of the night when I shake my fist at Him."

Saddened by her mother-in-law's continuing feud with the Lord, Ruth reached out and squeezed her hand. "He is good, and He loves us. I wish ye'd try to remember that."

Noemie squeezed her hand back. "I will try."

Changing the subject, Ruth glanced down the hill at the field. "What now? Chores, I mean."

Noemie exhaled as if the list were a mile long. "I was thinking we could get Bear to take down all the shutters so we can paint them. Whole house needs painting, too. Springhouse needs a new door. Root cellar needs cleaning. Axles on the wagon need greasing. Oh, I want Bear to run some new fence on the parcel up near the north property line—"

"Noemie, don't ye think the boy should live here rather than going back to Montgomery's every night?"

"I toyed with the idea. If you approve, I'll ask."

"I heard something prowling about last night."

"Me, too. Sent the chickens into a tizzy. I didn't see nothin', though."

"What do ye think?"

"I think it coulda been that bear Leroy mentioned."

"Speaking of, I know he's just a boy—"

"The size of two men." Noemie huffed a sigh. "And I'm no quivering daisy—"

"To say the least."

She shot Ruth the stink eye, but continued. "I'm not scared, but I get what we're dancing around here. I'd feel some better having a man around, too. I won't deny it." The sound of a shotgun firing somewhere in the woods echoed down through their valley and the women exchanged looks. "Hunters, but on my land." She rose, Ruth with her. "I'll get my gun."

———

THE TWO OF them had barely made it a quarter of a mile from the house when they spotted Bear emerging from the woods. He turned his horse toward them, proudly raised up a turkey, and trotted over. "I spotted a flock on the way home and thought you might like one."

Ruth noted he had two more of the birds hanging from the saddle. "Thank you, Bear." Pleased for a change in her diet, she took the tom from him and hung it on her saddle horn.

"Appreciate it, son." Noemie's expression turned thoughtful. "Ask Montgomery to stop by and see me sometime tomorrow, please?"

"Sure thing." The bird handed off, he nodded at the ladies and skedaddled out for home.

"Ye think he'll want to stay with us?" Ruth asked.

"We'll ask them both tomorrow."

SUNSET WAS Ruth's favorite time of day. She wandered along the fence that led out to the biggest part of the pasture and waited with anticipation. In the fading light, a glow flashed, disappeared, came again, and she pressed her fingers over her mouth in awe. An instant later, dozens more *lightnin' bugs*, as Noemie called them, rose up out of the grass, dancing, blinking, calling to mates. They left Ruth breathless, and she wondered if this was where the legend of faeries had come from.

Oh, Lord, I see the beauty of the works of Your hand so readily in this place...

She was delighted she'd come here with Noemie. Oconee County was beautiful. It felt like home to her. The thought made her wonder about her future, though. Would she marry again? She wanted children. How she wished they could have been Noemie's grandchildren—

"Good evening."

Ruth gasped and spun. Montgomery. She laid a hand to her chest and laughed. "Good Lord, ye gave me a fright."

He ducked his chin, embarrassed. "I'm sorry. Didn't mean to startle you."

"No, no. Twas I, lost in thought." She leaned on a fence post. "The ruminations of a foolish girl."

Montgomery, hands in his pockets, stepped past her and gazed out at the valley. "That view can give a person a lot to think about." He smiled at her over his shoulder. "I doubt whatever you were thinking was foolish."

To her surprise, Ruth felt her cheeks warm under his kind gaze. He had lovely blue eyes, intense, warm, inviting. "Did ye speak with Noemie?"

"No, I knocked, but no one answered. Then I saw you down here."

"She must still be in the tub."

"Do you know what she wanted to see me about?"

Ruth wondered if it was her place to discuss Bear, but then thought Noemie wouldn't mind, since both women were in agreement. "I believe she wanted to ask if we could have Bear."

Montgomery chuckled and turned to her. "He isn't exactly mine to give, but—"

"We did ask him today if he'd be willing to come live with us, and he said yes. But we had to make sure ye wouldn't mind."

"I hate to lose Bear. He's a good hand." He grinned at her. "But he spoke with me about the situation a little while ago, and I gave him my blessing. Besides, I think you need him more than I do."

"He's a dear boy and we enjoy his company. He's very helpful, of course. Sacks of feed I can't even roll, he tosses them about like they're stuffed with feathers."

"Yes, he's as strong as an ox." Montgomery kicked a pebble around with the toe of his boot, his expression darkening. "I'd prefer you two have a man around, anyway. And his pa won't mind."

"He's mentioned his family a time or two. They're close, but he doesn't live with them."

"Dall, his father, is the tailor in town, but Bear hated the work. Long as he has a job that gives him room and board, he doesn't have to be in the shop."

"He's a happy rascal doing farm chores. One day he'll have his own place. I'm sure of it." For some reason, this made her think of Leroy Heyward's visit. A repugnant man.

"What's that look for?"

"Oh, I was thinking of Mr. Heyward's visit the other day. The kindest thing I can say about him is that he's persistent. And nosy."

"Came asking a lot of questions, did he?"

"Aye, and he offered to buy the place. Noemie, however, is still quite angry with him. Hence our pen containing a hog."

Montgomery frowned with confusion.

"A peace offering from Mr. Heyward."

"Oh."

"I think he wasn't happy with all the help ye've given us. Every time Noemie said yer name, his face froze." Remembering the cold look in the man's beady eyes caused a chill to climb her spine and she rubbed her arms against the goosebumps.

Without a word, Montgomery peeled out of his coat

and draped it around Ruth's shoulders. She looked up into his handsome, weathered face, alight with a tender expression. For an instant, time seemed to stop, allowing them to hold each other's gaze. Then he blinked and stepped away. "Sun's down. Temperature drops quick."

"Thank you." Ruth hugged the coat tighter and breathed in the smoky scent of tobacco, a hint of oatmeal soap, and the aroma of something uniquely Montgomery Boaze, earthy and peaceful.

He cleared his throat and inched a little farther away from her. "You think she's drowned?"

"Quite possibly." They started walking toward the house. "Mr. Heyward said there is a bear sneaking about in the valley. We should be wary."

Montgomery's steps slowed, and Ruth took note of it. "Bear?" he repeated. "No. I hadn't heard of one recently. There are a few around, but they don't usually cause too much trouble."

"Oh."

"There's that look again."

Ruth never was very good at hiding her thoughts. She'd had to work very hard the other day in Mr. Heyward's presence to keep her brow from knitting and her mouth from tightening. Now she'd let a concern slip.

Well, Lord, I'm tired of keeping it to myself, and I trust Montgomery.

She stopped abruptly and turned to him. "I do think I saw someone in the kitchen that night. And I think someone has been making the rounds of our farm in the wee hours. I'm not a jittery female—well, I am a little—but I sense someone here about at times."

"Have you said anything to Noemie?"

"No, I don't want to spook her. If she were to shoot an unarmed vagrant, I'd feel terrible."

"Two women alone could make a vagrant—or deserter —mighty cocky."

"I suppose, yes."

"In any event, I told Bear to go ahead and gather his things and move in here. He'll be back anytime now."

Ruth let out a breath. "That makes me feel some better. I'm used to the city. Sometimes, the nights here are unbearably quiet...and lonely."

His face softened and she suspected, as a widower himself, he knew exactly what she meant. He nodded then pointed at the mountain closest to the farmhouse. "There's a rough trail over that pass. Instead of my farm being three miles away by the road, it's one. I'll show you sometime."

"All right, yes. I'd like that." Between being closer to Montgomery by a trail and knowing Bear would be in the house, Ruth thought she might sleep more peacefully that night than she had in months.

———

BEAR ARRIVED JUST as Montgomery was leaving. Ruth and Noemie settled the boy into the spare bedroom on the first floor. He placed his hunting rifle on the rack near the door. The ladies had seen his skill with it and were comforted by his presence. When Ruth's head touched the pillow, however, she wasn't thinking about the young man downstairs who had promised to watch over them.

She was thinking about the older gentleman with kind eyes, only a mile away by a walk along a mountain trail...

———

MONTGOMERY SAT DOWN and stared at the empty fireplace. Torturing himself, he let his mind wander down a path strewn with memories. His beautiful, sweet Maddie Sue sitting across from him. Firelight flickering off her golden hair as she knit, read the Bible, nursed their son. How many nights at this hearth had they talked of their future, listened intently to Bryl's babbled stories of frog-catching and fishing? Or the night they'd held hands and listened to their son share his heart on coming to the Lord.

Then it was only the two of them, Bryl growing into manhood, sitting in his mother's seat. From where he had shared his decision to attend West Point.

Montgomery patted the arm of the chair as if it were an old friend. So many memories, so much life lived from this spot.

Except for the past two years.

Alone, his mundane life was interrupted only here and there by a rare but treasured visit from his son. Now, with the war raging, he wondered if he would ever see Bryl again.

He leaned back with a heavy sigh. *Lord, keep him safe, please. Bring him home. Fill my house with the laughter and warmth of a family, of grandchildren...*

A deep, bone-chilling loneliness washed over Montgomery and, not surprisingly, he thought of Ruth. He hated how often his thoughts drifted to the young woman. He had no business, of course, thinking about her. He was nearly old enough to be her father. It was ridiculous. Yet, he found himself at odd times ruminating on her beauty, smiling over her fierce loyalty to Noemie, daydreaming about being near her.

He growled at his foolishness and rose to his feet. *Lord, take the woman off my mind, please. I'm merely lonely and she is attractive and kind. Any man would be drawn to her.* " Darla, I'm off to bed. Good evening."

"All right," she called from the kitchen. "You have a good evening, too, Mr. Boaze."

He sighed, doubting his sleep would be restful.

———

RUTH AWOKE before dawn and lengthened into a luxurious stretch before crawling from bed to dress. Humming softly to herself, she went straight to the kitchen and made the coffee, still humming, but the sticky July morning challenged her mood.

As she pumped water into the coffee pot, she marveled a little over her disposition, smiling inwardly. Her heart felt lighter today than it had in a long time. She lit the stove and set the pot on top of it.

Healing. Her heart was healing. More than that, she found it easy to count her blessings here. She felt, like Noemie, that this place was home. The crops were doing well. Rain came when needed. The cattle were getting fat and sassy. There was good, steady work to be done, and what she put her hand to mattered to the lifeblood of this farm. Bear was even teaching her the skills necessary to move the cattle about. Montgomery, she could tell, was proud of them. Aye, she was truly glad she'd come to Oconee County with Noemie.

Still humming, she grabbed the egg basket and went to gather a few for breakfast. It puzzled her that the chickens didn't seem to be producing as well as they had at first. A few of the nests had been empty two days in a row. Could they have a snake crawling into the coop? As she trudged toward it, lost in thought, she absently noted that Priscilla the hog was quiet this morning.

Ruth gathered up half a dozen eggs and headed back to the house when something about Priscilla's pen struck her. The animal was usually visible and quite vocal, snorting and pawing for a bucket of slop. She couldn't see the hog at all. The enclosure was a hundred yards away from the house and had a small shed in it. Priscilla, Ruth assumed, was lying inside in the shade. Still, no rooting about in the coolness of the morning? No venturing out to see if Ruth had a treat for her?

The departure from normal activity was marked. Ruth decided to make a quick check on the animal and strode down the hill. Upon her approach, she at first saw nothing amiss...then the stain seeping from the shadows kicked her heart up to a gallop. "Priscilla?" Silence.

A crawling fear wiggled in Ruth's gut. It wasn't wise to step into the pen with a moody hog, but that stain...and the silence. A fly buzzed and darted out of the shed. Ruth set down the basket of eggs and climbed over the fence. A few more steps and she saw the animal's legs poking out from the deeper shadows of the shed. In her heart, she knew Priscilla was dead, but she had to know how.

The bear? A panther? Explanations ricocheted through her mind and she stepped underneath the shed's roof. Priscilla lay spread out on the ground, no marks on her body other than a clean, murderous slice across her throat...

CHAPTER TEN

"Do ye think it was Mr. Heyward?" Ruth asked.

Beside her, Noemie, Bear, and Montgomery stared down at Priscilla's cold body. A ho rde of flies swarmed about the animal. Noemie shook her head. "Why would he give us a hog just to kill it?"

Ruth had no answer. It didn't make sense. "A deserter, then?"

"Why kill it and not take any meat?" Montgomery wondered aloud.

"Perhaps something startled him away before he could," Ruth said.

Montgomery looked at Bear. "You're sure you didn't hear anything last night?"

"No, sir. My room is in the back of the house, but I slept with the window down. Whoever did this was quiet."

Montgomery kneeled down and studied the ground. "Looks like the killer brushed his tracks away."

"That's odd," Noemie said. "Startled away, but had the time to clear his tracks?"

A thought came to Ruth. She was hesitant to voice it, but tossed it out after a moment. "What if it's some kind of warning?"

Montgomery rose, planted both hands on his hips. "Warning?"

"Mr. Heyward seemed intent on acquiring the farm. Mayhap he's playing both sides. A gift to make him look helpful *and* a way to throw a scare into us."

Montgomery huffed a sigh and regarded the hog with pity. "I wouldn't put anything past him, but that almost seems obvious."

"Well, maybe I need to go pay him a visit." Noemie's voice was hard and cold.

"How about you let me talk to him this time, Noemie?" Montgomery laid a hand on her shoulder. "You and your shotgun together make me nervous."

She grinned up at him. "Then how do you think Leroy feels?"

"Maybe he'd be more inclined to talk if he's not in fear for his life?"

The little woman scrunched her face in disapproval. "Fine. You could have a point." She snatched her gaze back to the hog. "In the meantime, I'm not about to let this meat spoil."

———

MONTGOMERY HATED anything to do with Leroy Heyward, but he especially hated the fact that he kept slaves. A tall, slender black man answered the door at Heyward's home and offered Montgomery a questioning gaze. "Yes, suh?"

"Leroy here?" He realized he had let his irritation lace

his voice and he tried again politely. "I mean, is he available?"

"I will check, suh." The man started to turn but stopped. "You Mr. Boaze, ain't you?"

"Yes, I am."

Something in the man's face relaxed, warmed. "Come on in and I'll see what he's up to. You wanna wait in the library?" He motioned to a room off to his right. Montgomery nodded and they parted for different directions. A few minutes later, Leroy strode into the room, a snifter of what smelled like brandy in his hand.

"Well, what brings you by my humble abode?"

Montgomery set down a glass knick-knack he'd been fumbling with and faced him. "Somebody killed that hog you gave Noemie."

Leroy's face went slack. "What? What are you talking about, *killed it?* "

"Slit her throat, right there in the hog pen." Montgomery glared, hoping the look made his point.

"Surely you don't think I did it? I gave her that hog. It was a prime animal, close to eight hundred pounds."

"Then, who?"

"Why are you asking me? Why do you think I know anything about it? Why couldn't it have been a deserter?"

Montgomery studied Leroy's clean-shaven, weathered face, pomade glistening in his dark, gra y-streaked hair. The fancy suit. Shiny shoes. All rouge on a pig. "I'll make this real clear to you, Leroy. You and I have been butting heads for a while now, but I don't know why exactly. Some misguided jealousy on your part, I think. But this changes things. Anything happens to those women, you'll dredge up a side of me you haven't seen in twenty years. And I'll come for you."

Leroy's eyes widened. Montgomery knew reputations —good and bad—took a long time to die. Bad ones were never really forgotten, just tucked away in people's memories.

He tapped Leroy on the chest. "I've worked hard to become the peaceable man I am. But I won't let anyone hurt Noemie and Ruth. No one."

"Save your wrath for somebody who deserves it, Boaze. You're barking up the wrong tree here."

"Maybe...maybe. You'd better hope so."

———

MONTGOMERY CLIMBED up in his wagon and sat a moment, collecting his wits, calming himself. *I believe he's behind this, Lord. I ask that You protect Ruth and Noemie and help me stay calm, but alert and wise. He's up to something. I know it...*

Montgomery finished his errands in town, picking up supplies and a new shipment of tools from the depot. He was stopped in front of the café, seriously considering a sandwich, when he caught sight of Leroy across the street. Slicing the air with vivid hand gestures, he was pointing north and talking to a young man Montgomery didn't know. About twenty, the greasy-headed kid was skinny, haggard, stuffed into a mismatched set of clothes that were too small for him.

The marks of a deserter.

Leroy shoved something into the kid's chest and stormed away. The stranger clutched the item close and ducked down the alley.

When did Leroy start giving money to panhandlers?

"Montgomery, my boy."

Montgomery looked over his shoulder. Mayor Fowler

ambled down the boardwalk, overdressed for the heat of the day in a nice suit and a new, brown stove pipe hat. His waxed mustache, however, was drooping a little. "Mayor."

"I'm glad I ran into you, Montgomery. Could you join me for lunch? I wanted to talk to you about the House agricultural bill."

He glanced back at Leroy, who was disappearing into the barbershop. The deserter had skedaddled. He shrugged mentally and pulled the brake. He had his suspicions about what he'd just seen transpire, but they were outright unsubstantiated. "Reckon I've got a few minutes. I don't support the bill, and we need to discuss it."

———

LUNCH WITH THE LONG-WINDED, glad-handing mayor had put a crimp in Montgomery's plans for the day, but that bill had to be stopped. Certain politicians needed to know Boaze wasn't keen on any political contributions till it was. As a result, he pulled up to his barn a good two hours later than he'd planned. He wouldn't get done half of what needed—

"I said get away from here!"

Darla's loud, angry voice from behind the house swung his attention back to his surroundings. He set the brake, leaped from the wagon, and rocketed to the backyard. Laundry and white sheets billowed in the wind. Behind one, he saw the clear silhouette of Darla's buxom figure and a man holding her arm. "Not another crumb," she yelled. "Now get along or I'll sic the law on ya!"

Montgomery didn't bother with the sheet. He dove into it and tackled the man to the ground. Taking advantage of his opponent's restricted movement, he pounded his face until flecks of blood seeped through the sheet.

Only then did Darla's screams break into his fury and he realized she was trying to pull him off the stranger. "Oh, Mr. Boaze, I'm so sorry! I'm so sorry! Please get off him. He's just hungry."

Bewildered, Montgomery climbed to his feet, swiped his hat off the ground, and backed away from the man.

"Oh, I'm so sorry, Mr. Boaze. I didn't mean—" Darla said as she pulled the sheet away from the stranger's face and helped him stand up. "He's just a boy, but I've told him he has to move on."

"What's going on here, Darla?"

She snatched the sheet back from the young man's dirty hands, and that was when Boaze recognized him. The mismatched, too-small suit and stringy hair. The deserter in town he'd seen speaking to Leroy.

"I asked what's going on here?"

Huffing, the boy wiped blood from his nose with the back of his hand. "I'm sorry, but I'm starvin—"

"And I told you not another crumb and you move on." She looked at Boaze, regret on her face. "I'm sorry. I should have sent him away, but I fed him lunch. Then he wanted a sack of leftovers. I didn't have anything else. I understand he's hungry and these boys don't think right when they're hungry, but—"

"Second deserter this month." Montgomery shook his head, angry over the situation and the choices he was being forced into. He saw fear but a sense of entitlement in the boy's scrawny, fuzzy face. "I saw you in town talking to Leroy Heyward."

"Who?"

"Tall, older fella, nice suit."

"Oh. Him. Didn't know his name. I, uh, just did some work for him...around one of his farms."

"Funny you should mention that. You can do some chores for your food here or move on."

"Chores?" the boy practically yelped.

"Yeah, if you can work for Leroy, you can work for us. I've got crops need weeding, animals that need to be fed and watered, repairs on my barn—"

The boy tossed up his hands. "I'll head back to town. Thank you just the same." The boy scrambled past them and double-timed it down the driveway.

Darla waited a moment before she spoke. "Thank you, Mr. Boaze. That was mighty gallant of you. I'm sorry for the trouble."

Montgomery flexed his right hand, surprised at his bloody knuckles. "My Christian charity ended here, Darla. Anymore deserters show up, you send them to me. Don't discuss it with them. Don't give them so much as a biscuit. They'll work for their food or move on."

"Yes, sir."

He turned and watched the boy's retreating figure. A butchered hog, a deserter manhandling Darla. This all felt connected somehow. A shadow was falling across Oconee County, but Montgomery couldn't discern who was casting it. Given time, he would.

———

IT WAS a little on the late side to be calling on Montgomery, but Leroy had a strong desire to cover his tracks better. Playing the victim couldn't hurt.

He knocked on the door and waited. A moment later, the curtain moved aside, and Darla's face turned plum near ash as recognition dawned. Leroy sucked on his teeth, annoyed by her less-than-warm reception, and wondered if she was going to open the door.

The lock clicked and the door cracked open about an inch. The woman regarded him with a narrow-eyed, suspicious gaze. "What are you doing here at this hour?"

He waved his hat in a vague apology. "Yeah, I know it's a little late, but I wanted to talk to Montgomery about Noemie's hog. Maybe I've got some leads."

"He's already in bed."

"Oh."

"You should go away and come back in the morning."

"You sure he's in bed? Maybe he's reading. You could see if he'd talk to me for a minute?"

She looked uncertain, chewed on her lip, finally nodded. "I'll see if his light's burning. If it's not, you go on home."

"Surely."

Hesitantly, she opened the door. "Wait in the parlor."

Leroy obeyed with a smile. Inwardly, he wanted to slap Darla into next Sunday. The scar in his forehead twitched as he idly wandered about the neat, prim sitting room. He ran his finger across the top of an end table. Not a lick of dust. Darla took good care of ol' Boaze.

Yet, she acted like just talking to Leroy Heyward was a distasteful chore and mighty inconvenient, to boot. He sure was tired of getting that uppity, scared look from her. What had he ever seen in the woman?

One thing he'd learned in the last few years was—

"His room is dark. I'll let him know you came by, though."

Leroy rubbed the scar on his head and turned to her. "You know, I was just thinking, I've learned a valuable lesson in the last several years, as I've bought up businesses and farms."

Darla tapped her foot impatiently and folded her arms across her chest. "And what's that?"

He ambled over to her, but veered to the right, planning to walk right on by her when the squiggly, jittering worms in his brain screamed. "I don't have to put up with anybody I don't like."

In one swift, lightning- fast movement, Leroy's hand snaked out, plucked a heavy, brass candlestick off the end table, and brought it across Darla's temple with a bone-cracking thud. The woman spun and drifted to the floor in a slow, graceful wilt.

Leroy examined the candlestick. *Huh. Didn't even get any blood on it.*

CHAPTER ELEVEN

LEROY SHIFTED HIS POSITION BEHIND THE LIVERY, SETTLING against a tall oak tree. A silver half-moon hung in the sky, and the cool, peaceful calm of the wee hours settled his singing nerves. Inside the barn, the horses, all fed and put up for the evening, nickered softly. He flicked his pocketknife open and commenced to cleaning the fresh dirt from his fingernails, more by touch than sight. It was a wonder his suit wasn't an unholy mess. Or maybe it was and he just couldn't see the dirt—and probably some blood—in the weak light.

He hadn't really meant to kill Darla. It had been so easy, though. She was there. The candlestick was there. Leroy had fortunately hit her just right, so she hadn't screamed or bled much at all. She'd just whirled and dropped like a dancer.

Would have been hell to pay if it had gone differently. If she'd screamed and woke up Boaze.

But she hadn't, and now Darla was dead and buried,

like a few of his other problems over the years. Burying always was the hard part.

Soft footfalls interrupted his reverie. Pushing away a speck of sadness over never having won the woman's heart, Leroy put his knife away and whistled softly. A shadowy figure stepped out of a grove of oaks and approached him.

"Again, good work on the hog." *Montgomery Boaze is fit to be tied, that's for sure.*

"Yes, sir." The soldier boy shrugged his skinny shoulders. "It sure seemed like a waste of a fine animal."

"But it sent a stronger message than a bunch of dead chickens would've."

The boy chuckled. "Not as much of a ruckus, either. The hog went down quiet. Only..."

"Only what?"

"I didn't get a chance to cut it up like you wanted. I heard something and got spooked."

"You failed to mention that earlier today." A massacred, bloody hog would have had a more chilling impact on Noemie and Ruth, easily inching them more toward selling out. The dead animal seemed to have disturbed Montgomery quite a lot, however. He was chomping at the bit to tie Leroy to it, but he wouldn't. Wouldn't tie him to Darla's sudden disappearance either.

Leroy almost laughed out loud as he reached into his pocket and produced a small velvet bag. "The rest of your fee. However..." He reached in and removed some coins but left behind a little something special. "You didn't make it bloody enough." He jangled the coins for fun and tossed it to the boy, who made a good catch in the dim light.

He bounced it in his palm once, still apparently satisfied with the weight. "Reckon that'll do."

"You still sleeping in Noemie's barn?"

"Mostly, yeah. I figure if I was to get discovered, I could overpower a woman easy and move on quick-like."

Leroy chuckled again but didn't bother to explain to the boy he'd be no match for Noemie. "Well...if I need you for anything else, I'll know where to find you."

———

RUTH CHEWED on her bottom lip and stared at the empty nesting box. Again, several hens either hadn't laid eggs or something was taking them. Should she bring it to Noemie's attention? She gathered up only five eggs and started back toward the house when Winnie and Dollar, their mares, grumbled, ready to be fed and let out to pasture. From their stall windows, they were watching Ruth with hope-filled eyes.

"All right, all right, I can't stand the way ye're looking at me." Ruth set the basket of eggs on the ground by the gate and slipped inside the fence that surrounded the barn. The horses grumbled again. "I'm coming, I'm coming..." She marched down the breezeway and stopped abruptly.

A scent—no, an odor—unpleasant, foul, hit her hard. The hair stood up on her arms and a breath of air stirred on her neck. She began to turn when a hand snaked out of the shadows and covered her mouth. An arm wrapped around her waist.

Ruth screamed, but the sound was muffled, pointless.

"Please, ma'am, don't scream."

A man's voice in her ear. Ruth wiggled harder and tried to cry aloud, but the sound was lost. T he smell of his unwashed body made her want to wretch.

"Please, I really don't mean you no harm. I'm letting go."

True to his word, the man released Ruth and jumped back with his hands up. "I'm sorry, I'm sorry."

Ruth whirled on the intruder, a slender fella in a worn suit that was too short for him. Her heart was in her throat. She could barely breathe, then the air rushed back at once. "What do ye mean grabbing me like that if ye meant me no harm?" Her eyes darted about and she snatched a pitchfork from the wall. She pointed the tongs at him, and the young man raised his hands higher. "Explain yerself," she demanded.

"I just didn't want you to scream. I wanted to prove I mean ya no harm."

Ruth scrutinized the man with severity. "What are ye doing hiding in our barn?"

Sheepishly, he pulled three eggs from his pocket. "I was hungry."

Ruth didn't know what to think. He *had* let her go. A noise from behind her tempted her to look, but she resisted, and an instant later, Bear was beside her with his rifle raised at the intruder. "Miss Ruth, you all right?"

Was she? Had fear made her overly suspicious in these trying times? He had let her go. Oh, where was her Christian charity? She pushed Bear's barrel down. "Could ye eat a good breakfast?"

The man's eyes lit up. "I surely could, ma'am."

"All right. One meal and ye're on your way. Agreed?"

"Agreed."

Now...as long as Noemie didn't get *her* gun.

MONTGOMERY STRODE down the steps with an undeniably light step. He chided himself for it, but he had decided Noemie and Ruth should be warned about Darla's deserter, and he was looking forward to another visit with the ladies. He burst into the kitchen, prepared for breakfast and to tell his housekeeper of his plans.

Only, Darla was not in the kitchen. Neither had she started breakfast. The stove was cold. The frying pan untouched. Had she gone somewhere? He didn't recall her saying anything about errands. Maybe she'd gone over to Noemie's for a visit. It seemed unlikely, but it was as good a place as any to start looking for her. Especially since he was going there, anyway.

He saddled his favorite bay mare and took the short trail over. He hadn't been this way in years. As the morning sun flickered through the scotch pines and mountain laurel, he guided the horse carefully over the rocky ground, around mammoth boulders, and over a couple of small creeks. The trail was overgrown and washed out in places, but passable. He thought he might send a hand up here to clean it up a little more. Nothing wrong with having a quicker route to Noemie's.

Half an hour later, he emerged from the woods, trotted across the pasture, and tied his horse to the hitching post out front. He knocked on the screen door expectantly, but the ladies didn't answer. He listened for a moment and picked up the muffled sound of voices—two male voices, he was sure of it, mixed with Noemie and Ruth's.

He took a few steps down the porch and listened at the canvas-covered window for a moment.

"Aw, thanks, ma'am, that's the most food I've seen in months."

Montgomery didn't recognize this voice.

"Miss Noemie sure makes good flapjacks, Thomas. I'll go out to the spring house and get us some milk."

Montgomery knew Bear's voice, but who was this other man, Thomas? Puzzled, Montgomery cleared his throat and called, "Noemie, Ruth, I'm coming in, if I may?"

"Come ahead," Noemie replied.

Montgomery went back to the door and was reaching for the screen when Ruth appeared, rushed and a little breathless. She opened it for him and greeted him with a smile that made his heart—well, he thought it actually skipped a beat. She had perfect, soft, kissable lips.

"Good mornin', sir. Join us for breakfast?"

He snatched off his hat. "I was hoping you might ask." He walked with her toward the kitchen. "Seeing as how I can't find my housekeeper, I am a little hungry. And I wanted to let you know—" He practically skidded to a stop. The boy who had been harassing Darla sat at Noemie's table, his cheeks stuffed with food, half a dozen flapjacks and bacon covering the plate before him.

Noemie looked up from the pan of frying bacon she was tending and frowned. "What's the matter, Montgomery? Is he in your seat?"

"I ran him off my place yesterday."

The boy gulped down his food, nearly choking on it. His eyes widened and his gaze ricocheted around the room.

"He had his hands on Darla, was arguing with her about more food. Seems he doesn't take no very well."

Noemie moved the bacon from the heat and turned to the men. "Is Darla all right?"

"Well, now, that's just the thing..." Montgomery moved around the table, positioning himself between this stranger and the women. "Darla wasn't anywhere to be found this morning. I thought she might be here."

Ruth and Noemie exchanged glances, shook their

heads. Noemie stepped over beside Montgomery, still holding her spatula. "I ain't seen her." She leveled a suspicious gaze on the breakfast guest. "She didn't tell you where she was going?"

"She didn't mention she was going anywhere. Horse wasn't gone, but sometimes she walks over to Moss's Orchard. Even if she does leave early, she makes sure breakfast is on the stove for me. It was cold. Never even lit a fire."

Noemie's stare drilled into the boy. "You know anything about this?"

He stood up slowly. "No, ma'am. Last I saw his housekeeper was yesterday."

"Ye're the one," Ruth said. "You've been stealing eggs all along, haven't ye?"

"You said you were going back to town," Montgomery reminded him.

The boy licked his lips and raised his hands. "I did. That fella in town, he's the one who told me your two farms were good places to hang around."

Montgomery felt a flush of anger heat his face. "Leroy Heyward. He sent you out here."

The boy's face picked up an edge, tension in his muscles revealing fear and anger. "I told you, I don't know his name."

"Did ye kill our hog, too?" Ruth asked.

"Empty your pockets, boy," Montgomery ordered as his hand landed on the revolver at his hip. "Slowly."

Thomas frowned but slowly dug into his right pocket, emerged with a handful of items, and dropped them on the table. "Aint much. My pocketknife and a little spare change I picked up here and there."

A wave of molten fury washed over Montgomery as he

recognized a piece of jewelry among the booty. He shifted coins out of the way and plucked a round, gold locket from the grouping. His gut twisted. "Where did you get this?"

The stranger's eyes widened. "I didn't take that."

Montgomery was on the boy as fast as a panther, grabbing his collar, nearly raising him off his feet. "I asked where did you get this?" He shook the kid. "It belongs to my housekeeper." He was yelling, shaking him violently. "Where is Darla?"

"I don't know what you're talking about."

The two men's gazes locked. Sneering at him, livid over the lies, Montgomery shook him one last time and released him. "If you don't know where she's at, how'd you get her locket?"

Thomas's countenance changed suddenly, all signs of a frightened victim fleeing, leaving behind the look of a young man who was as comfortable with trouble as he was with lying. In a blur of motion, he flipped over the table, sending food and cutlery crashing to the floor.

He dashed past them toward freedom, but Montgomery reached out, swung Thomas around, and almost had a good grip on him when he slipped on a smattering of scrambled eggs. The boy took advantage of the shifting balance and swung at Montgomery. The blow glanced off his cheek, but he managed to grab Thomas's shoulders. The two grappled, twisted, and threw punches. Montgomery blocked a strike, tried for his own, and somehow, he and the boy went tumbling out the canvas-covered window on to the porch.

They fought for a moment through the tangle of the cloth, then Montgomery managed a well-aimed, ferocious punch to the boy's head. It should have rung the lad's bell, but he shook it off and hit Montgomery with a painful uppercut, snapping his head back.

His anger at this worthless, deceitful lay-about in full flame now, Montgomery blocked a blow, delivered one of his own, but the boy came back with a strike to Montgomery's ribs. Seeing red, he tackled the boy and they rolled off the porch into the yard, still exchanging blows.

They tumbled about in the grass for a second, then managed to gain their feet. Montgomery's arms felt like hundred-pound sacks of wet feed. His chest hurt from sucking wind. A seed of worry sprouted in his mind. Was he energetic enough to take this boy? He sensed the women behind him and knew he had no choice—

The ear-splitting peel of thunder from a shotgun boomed over them. Both men froze with their fists raised. Chests heaving, they glared at one another, blood trickling from noses and mouths. "That'll be enough, gentlemen," Ruth commanded.

Montgomery shifted enough to see her on the front porch holding Noemie's shotgun on them. Fearless. Determined.

She was magnificent.

Thomas spat blood and grinned up at her. "You fire a scatter gun from there you'll kill us both."

Noemie stepped from behind Ruth and raised her Colt Dragoon, cocking it as she leveled it on the boy's forehead. Her hand was eerily steady. "I fire from here, I'll just kill you."

A jarring, metallic, clattering noise jolted Montgomery out of his fog and he stepped further away from the line of fire. Bear stood on the end of the porch, mouth agape, eyes round as full moons, an upset pail and a puddle of milk at his feet.

CHAPTER TWELVE

THE JAIL CELL BARS CLANGED SHUT AND SHERIFF HOLDEN shook his head at the new guest. "This is plain turning into a revolving door. Just released one of your friends this morning."

"I don't have any friends here."

The sheriff smiled knowingly at Montgomery. "Yeah, all these boys travel alone." Sarcasm dripped from his tongue. "Fact is, they're too scared to fight and they're too scared to run off by themselves." An older gentleman with a barrel chest and icy blue eyes, he leveled a hard stare at Thomas, now occupying the cell. "I'm gonna hold you for three days—unless we find Darla before then and she either clears you or..." He trailed off.

Thomas sat on the cot, resting his back against the wall. "I swear I didn't hurt her. And I don't know anything about that locket." He shook his head, his expression perplexed. "I can't explain it."

His answer troubled Montgomery. It was a terrible

defense...or the truth. "You said you were coming back to town, but then I find you at Noemie's."

"I came back in, but nobody in town was feeling particularly generous. I had a couple of drinks and then walked back out to the place on Frying Pan Ridge."

"Anybody see you?"

"Nah. It was one or two this morning. Nobody was out."

"That's convenient." Montgomery was beginning to lean toward hanging this boy. He looked guilty as sin, but Montgomery couldn't ignore the link to Leroy and his infatuation with Darla. Montgomery sighed, frustrated, angry, sick over her disappearance. With each passing minute, he had less and less hope. He turned to the sheriff. "I'll head back and make sure the boys go over my property with a fine-tooth comb. If she's there, we'll find her."

"Give me a few hours to round up some riders and we'll help you look. We don't find her, we'll run a raid on Tunnel Hill." He tilted his head and studied Thomas for a moment. "You got friends up there?"

"I told you, I don't have any friends."

———

AFTER LEAVING Thomas with the marshal, Montgomery stopped by his farm. Still no Darla. Billy Rafferty, his foreman, hadn't seen her, heard her, or come across any sign of a struggle. Worry gnawing at him like a rat, Montgomery asked all the farmhands to check the property again. The henhouse, outhouse, doghouse, smokehouse, and springhouse were inspected carefully. Three hands walked the entire fence line.

Nothing.

Montgomery and Rafferty rode out in opposite directions and knocked on the door of every farm within five miles.

Again, nothing.

None of Darla's clothes were missing. Her room had not been disturbed. Her bed did not appear to have been slept in.

Montgomery's spirits sank lower. It was as if the woman had vanished into thin air, and that wasn't possible. Still, he kept his men looking for another three days, walking the woods, riding the trails. Nothing. Not a shred of cloth, nothing.

Now, he settled at Noemie's table and stared listlessly at a steaming slice of Shepherd's pie. "Like she walked out the door and stepped off the edge of the world."

Ruth sat down across from him. "Is there any chance she had a lover and she snuck off with him?"

"Everyone says no, or at least not that they knew of."

Noemie joined them and dished herself a serving. "So that boy that was here, he never fessed up to anything?"

"Swore all the way to town he never touched your hog and he didn't know how that locket wound up on him. The last time he saw Darla was when I threw him off the property."

"You believe him?"

Montgomery thought long and hard as he poked at the pie. His mind circled back to Leroy and the man's accusations that Darla was more than a housekeeper. "Somebody's lying. Either that boy or Heyward. Heyward swore up and down he hadn't seen Darla in days."

A somber silence blanketed the group and they poked at their food for several minutes. Finally, Noemie wondered aloud, "The deserter makes the most sense. You said you caught him red-handed getting violent with Darla. No telling what that fella's been up to."

It made sense, Montgomery knew. And the boy had been hanging around here as well, stealing eggs, according to Ruth. If he'd own up to it, Montgomery could find peace. As it was, "I still feel like I should be looking for her." He let his gaze drift out the window over the sink, up to the mountains, "that she's out there somewhere."

Ruth patted his hand. "Ye've done all ye could do."

He smiled sadly at her. "Maybe. I was going to look over the trail back to my place one more time. Why don't you let me take you, show it to you?" He cleared his throat and added, "You, too, Noemie. You should know where the trail is."

She shot him a stink eye. "You act like I didn't grow up here, Montgomery. Like I didn't know Luke his whole life. I know where your trail is. Used to stop at the spring on top of the mountain for a sip of water. Show Ruth, though, in case she ever needs to hotfoot it over to your place."

"What about Bear?" Ruth asked.

"He knows the trail," Montgomery said.

"Besides, he's finishing that fence down by the shed."

Did Ruth's question mean she didn't want to go? She didn't want to be alone with Montgomery? " But if you're busy, Ruth, we can go some other—"

"No, no. A ride would be lovely."

"In fact, you two scoot after supper," Noemie said. "I'll get the dishes."

———

A LITTLE WHILE LATER, Montgomery and Ruth were astride Lucille, his mare, jogging across the field and heading up the trail. Being a short ride, they'd opted to double-up on her.

As the horse negotiated her way around a thick stand of laurel, Ruth asked, "Did you put this here?"

"No, it was an old Indian trail before we ever came along. My ma used to take it to come visit Noemie's mother-in-law. They were good friends."

As the horse climbed and skittered around boulders, following the steep, slightly overgrown path, Montgomery tried to focus on the scent of moist earth and rhododendron in the air. Otherwise, he would be too preoccupied by the delicate arms wrapped around his waist, the warm curves pressed into his back. What had he been thinking to make this ride?

That she may need help in a hurry should another drifter come along. Now get your mind on your business, he scolded. *You're almost old enough to be the woman's father.*

But the *almost* echoed around in his brain...

"I hope by some miracle Darla reappears. Could she be lost in the woods? I know that might sound foolish..."

He sighed. "No. Stranger things have happened." And he'd give his eyeteeth for a miracle now. *Where did she go, Lord? I pray she's all right.*

A few minutes later, they topped the ridge of the mountain and Montgomery pointed down at his house through the pines, a quarter-mile off. "It's easy from here. The trail is clear." He hated to turn around so soon, but didn't have an excuse to dally—

"Oh, might I have a sip of water?" Ruth had spotted the little spring that flowed from the mountain and dripped over the edge of a rock. "And, look, there's a ladle." She slid off from behind him and hurried over to it.

"There's been one there long as I can remember. The

last one was about rusted through, so I replaced it." He drummed his fingers on the saddle horn as she held the scoop beneath the water and let it fill.

Should he get off?

"My, that's cold and refreshing. Would ye like a sip?"

With the invitation, he dismounted and walked over, trailing the horse. Their fingers touched and their gazes held.

You're forty years old, Montgomery, a voice bellowed at him.

He winced and took the ladle. "Thank you."

Ruth turned and wandered over to the shoulder of the trail, scanning the view of his home. "Yer farm is lovely, especially from here." The shadows were growing long, and he knew, creeping over his spread. Evening on his farm. He put the ladle back on its ledge and joined her. Rafferty and another hand, maybe George, rode the hay wagon over to the sheep pen. They and the driver immediately started shucking hay in with the animals. The last chore of the evening.

He felt guilty. He'd scanned the trail as they'd ridden up it, again looking for any sign of Darla, but, admittedly, his attention had been divided.

"How long did ye say your wife has been gone?" she asked gently.

"Five years."

"Many men would not have kept up their home after such a loss. I'm glad to see ye have paid it heed."

"Maddie Sue loved our place. She planted those roses over there "— he pointed at the backyard— "and the magnolia in the front yard."

"Why is it ye've not moved on? Not remarried? If ye'll pardon me for asking."

Montgomery rested his hand on the butt of the .44 at his hip and shrugged. "I don't reckon I've quit looking, it's just no one's..." he faded off and glanced down at her. "No one's come along that piqued my interest." *And you're a liar, Montgomery Boaze.*

"Did ye have a good marriage?"

His surprise at her questions must have shown on his face. She kicked a rock and turned away from him. "I'm sorry. It's none of me business." She drifted over to a boulder and sat down. Montgomery had the feeling there was something she wanted to say. Curious, he wanted to hear it, so he answered.

"Yes. Maddie Sue was the sunshine in my life. Everything good and joyous and beautiful that makes a man smile, she embodied it. I loved her as much the day she died as the day I asked her to marry me. Maybe more."

Ruth sighed and leaned forward, propping her chin in her hands. "I don't know what that's like."

"You saying you didn't have a good marriage? I thought James was a good man."

"James was, more accurately, a busy man. Busy with everything but his wife. I suppose that's why Noemie and I are so close. We've spent a lot of time together."

Montgomery didn't know what to say. He wasn't quite sure what Ruth was confessing, if she was confessing anything at all.

"James traveled quite a bit for his father. Business trips took him away often, for weeks at a time. Then, when the war came, he enlisted. The last two years, I saw him once. I grieve his loss, but I..." She stopped, shook her head, and started again. "Honestly, I think I grieve more for Noemie. She lost a son. I lost a stranger. And it makes me feel terrible."

Montgomery took a moment to sort through the confession...and the way he felt about it. No denying it, the fact that she wasn't as much a grieving widow as he'd thought lightened his heart. He knew that pain and didn't wish it on anyone. On impulse, he dropped Lucille's reins, ambled over, and sat down beside her.

"I don't think you should feel guilty. You can't help how you feel. And James was clearly a fool."

She looked up and her glimmering, deep brown eyes—eyes the color of polished mahogany—ignited a spark in his chest.

"Why do ye say that?"

He looked away, afraid she might see right into his soul. "Marriage is no different than any other relationship. You don't nurture it, it won't grow. Love will dry up and blow away."

"That's how I feel. Now that the shock has worn off, I feel dry and empty. I wonder if I'll ever...or if I'll wind up like you." She raised a hand as if he might protest the perceived insult. "No offense. I only mean, I don't want to give up, quit looking, quit hoping."

"You think that's what I've done?" He was taken aback by the idea.

"Ye're a handsome man with a fine home and grand farm. Surely, there's been a woman somewhere who could have touched yer heart."

Montgomery leaned down and picked up a stick. He tapped his palm with it as he thought, as he digested her observations. The last five years almost seemed like a fuzzy photograph with spots of clarity. Bryl being one of them. Perhaps he *had* given up, settling into a certain comfort in his solitude.

He didn't want that to happen to Ruth. "You're beautiful

and kind, Ruth. Smart as a whip." He rose, retrieved his horse, and looked at her across the saddle. "Not a lot of men around now, but when the war is over, there'll be a lot of young bucks tripping over themselves to court you." And Montgomery made up his mind right then, he would fall on his sword to see it happen. Because her happiness mattered to him. "Let's head back."

―――

NOEMIE PEERED out her kitchen window, watching the trail. When Boaze and Ruth came shooting out from the trees, she reached into the sink of sudsy water and went to washing dishes with energy. "I probably shouldn't be throwing them at each other," she said aloud to no one, as she was not really interested in talking to the Lord, "but I want to see Ruth taken care of. She thinks I don't know, but James wasn't much of a husband, always off gallivanting around the east for his pa." She dipped a plate in the clean water. "He never cheated on her, but he sure took her for granted."

She was finishing up the dishes when the pair came in the back door, through the pantry, and into the kitchen. "Have a nice ride? Get the trail all figured out?"

"Aye. And we're close neighbors. Closer than I realized."

"Yeah, speaking of neighbors "— Montgomery fanned himself with his hat— "it doesn't seem entirely appropriate, what with Darla missing, but the town is having a barbecue next Friday night. A Fourth of July get-together. I wasn't of a mind to go—I never go, in fact." He glanced back and forth at them, then pinned his gaze on Noemie. "I'm going this time to talk with Senator Neeble about a farm bill. I think you two should go." He nudged his chin toward Ruth. "She could make some new friends, and you could see all the cousins you haven't run into yet."

Noemie suspected something about the invitation, that it wasn't as cut-and-dried as it sounded. But Montgomery had a point. Maybe he was looking to escort Ruth but couldn't ask outright? Wouldn't be able to for a while. There was the mourning period to observe, even if they weren't wearing black anymore. She fought the sadness in her heart, trying not to think about James. "I think we could swing a free Friday night."

"All right then." He smiled at them and dropped his hat in place. "Reckon I'd best get on home. It's getting late."

After he was gone, Noemie made a plate for Bear and set it on the stove. Ruth sat at the table, nursing a cup of coffee. Her gaze was all frosted and faraway. Noemie poured herself a cup and joined her. "What are you wool-gathering about?"

"I was pondering something Montgomery said. About the young bucks in this county. I feel as if ye're both conspiring to marry me off."

"Well, not tomorrow but..." she trailed off. The joke hurt more than it made her want to laugh. But what was that about young bucks? "He mentioned there's some around?"

"He said they'd knock themselves over to court me. He paid me a lovely compliment in the process."

Noemie tried not to be too curious or too eager, but she was both. "What did he say?"

"That I was beautiful and smart as a whip."

"All true." *And look at Montgomery noticing...*

Ruth smiled, a cautious tilt to her lips. "I don't know if I'm ready to meet anyone yet."

Noemie patted the back of her hand. "We'll stand off in

a corner by ourselves if you want, and you can look all these young bucks over from a distance, if that's how you want it. But you should get out, and I would enjoy seeing my people."

Ruth squeezed her hand. "Ye know I'll do anything for ye. We'll go to this "— she shrugged with the new word— "barbecue."

CHAPTER THIRTEEN

THE WEEK, FULL OF HARD WORK FROM SUNUP TO SUNDOWN, passed quickly. Friday came, and the girls gave themselves leeway to quit a little early in anticipation of the barbecue. "It'll be good for us," Noemie had said. "And all the chores will still be there tomorrow." Bear and Ruth had not argued with her.

Ruth smiled over the matter and examined her appearance in the bureau's mirror. Late evening sun streamed in the window and bathed her in an almost heavenly light, making her red dress glow. She pivoted and watched the skirt fly. Simple cotton with silk accents, the gown fit snugly and featured some detailed floral embroidery on the bodice, but she'd opted not to wear her voluminous hoop. Six petticoats gave her enough fluff but allowed her to navigate through a door.

"Ah, you're pretty as a picture," Noemie commented from the door. "You'll sure give the young bucks something to look at. And if there ain't any there, the old bucks'll notice."

―――――

THE BARBECUE WAS HELD at the large park in the center of town. The Downtown Business Association sponsored and served the barbecue. The aroma of roasting meat made her stomach rumble. On the edge of the park, vendors had set up booths selling everything from sparklers to beer. The ones selling alcohol had the longest lines of all. Torches and lamps burned everywhere, the celebration was bright and festive.

Ruth was pleased to see many of the women were not wearing hoops, quite a rebellious fashion statement, but Walhalla was a town less inclined to worry about convention than Silver Springs was. Around her, hundreds of voices carried on a steady, lighthearted hum. Several people quickly approached Noemie, hugged her with joy, which Ruth tried to emulate when she was introduced to these strangers. She truly desired to be the sparkling, devoted daughter-in-law.

The party grew tiresome quickly, however. New face after new face paraded across her path. Mostly older, mostly women. This cousin or that old friend kept Noemie bound up in non-stop conversation. A few young men, several not even old enough to enlist yet, did try to capture her attention and promised they'd return when the dancing started.

Ruth tried not to appear rude, but she barely listened to them as she surveyed the crowd...looking for Montgomery, her only friend besides Noemie. She reminded herself he'd most likely be as popular as her mother-in-law. Yes, she decided, the evening might relegate her to wallflower status unless she took up some of the promised dances.

Being a wallflower was more enticing.

The young men of marriageable age were either German and spoke very little English, or they were home on leave, recovering from wounds. Bandaged heads, arms in slings, crutches—for the life of her, Ruth had no idea how they intended to manage a dance. Their pride would make sure they tried. It seemed to her all these boys were too young to be soldiers. They were slender as grasshoppers and either bursting with swagger or rocking on their heels with shyness.

Men Montgomery's age were weathered by experience and wisdom. They were more poised, reserved, confident, but not prideful.

As if reading her mind, the crowd parted and Montgomery strode toward her, a warm smile on his face that brought out those creases around his eyes. She was taken aback for a moment by his spiffy appearance. No worn shirt or suspenders today. He was wearing a red silk vest, beige linen coat, pressed pants, and shined boots. He was breathtakingly handsome.

"Am I a sight?" he asked, tugging on the vest.

"You clean up all right," Noemie said, ending a conversation with yet another cousin and turning to Montgomery with her own grin.

He leaned back to appraise Ruth and Noemie. "You two are quite the delight, as well."

"We've had our share of attention this evening," Noemie agreed. "You might need to do a little filtering for Ruth here when the dancing starts. I don't know the riffraff from the do-wells."

"I'll do my best. In the meantime, I've got a table reserved for us and they're about to start serving." He offered both ladies an arm and strolled with them slowly through the guests, nodding here and there, raising an eyebrow now and again at certain people.

Ruth was puzzled by the slow escort and the open way people took note of the threesome. "I feel as if I'm on display." She looked up at him. "Like you're parading us."

Noemie flicked her fan open and subtly placed it in front of her face. "What's going on, Montgomery?"

He nodded and smiled at a young man who eyed the ladies, nodded in return at Montgomery, and then hurried past. "I got to thinking about the drifter on your property, and the hog, and I thought I should make some things plain to whoever might be watching. Plenty of scalawags on the fringe of this party."

"You didn't take us to raise."

Ruth heard the agitation in Noemie's voice and tried not to mirror it, but Ruth didn't care to be steered about like a horse, either. "It seems a bit obvious."

"Noemie asked me to help filter out the riffraff." He smiled at a group of young men in uniform. Home on leave, no doubt. Their gazes lingered on Ruth. "Riffraff," Montgomery dead panned.

A moment later, the three approached a table and Montgomery hurried to pull out the chairs for his charges. There was room for four more guests at the table. He glanced at the empty seats and then leaned toward the ladies, as if in a hurry to say his piece before anyone else joined them. "I know you two can take care of yourselves. And I know you've got Bear looking out for you. This is different." He glanced over at a group of boys in uniform, gathered around a beer wagon. "That's a rowdy bunch. Thankfully, they'll be leaving in a few days, but they're eyeing you pretty hard, Ruth. You needed to be seen with a man."

"I shouldn't have come."

"No...no." Noemie leaned back and held a glare on Montgomery for a moment but then let it go. "We're not gonna hide away."

"I'm not asking you to. All I'm saying is my presence around the prettiest girl here might make them look someplace else for a dance—or at least watch their manners. If not, I'm here to keep the peace."

Prettiest girl here? Ruth tried not to stumble over the compliment as it was most likely a simple observation. "Perhaps I shouldn't entertain their requests at all." She didn't want to.

"Decide your answer now. You dance with one of them, you'll have to dance with them all."

Ruth peered around Montgomery at the boys in gray, passing around a bottle of liquor. Where was the sheriff? Would he control them if they started to get out of hand? The last thing she wanted was for Montgomery to get hurt on account of her. Though, thinking back to Thomas, the deserter, he was capable of handling himself.

"Well, if they ask, I can say yes. That might be the best way to keep the peace. They've seen me with you, after all."

"Just tell them I'm your father."

Montgomery's face was inscrutable, but Ruth got the definite impression he was annoyed. By the soldiers? Or by the mistaken insinuation? "I didn't mean to imply anything about yer age."

"Let's not borrow trouble," Noemie said, watching the boys as well. "We'll enjoy the meal and when the music starts, Montgomery, take her for a turn. Or two."

About the time they finished their meal of barbecue pork, Mayor Fowler invited everyone through a megaphone to come enjoy the mountain sounds of Filo Foggarty and His Backwoods Boys. The crowd around them roared with approval.

And when they started to play, Ruth marveled over the music coming from the quartet. Four elderly men with ridiculously long beards played banjos, fiddles, and a dulcimer as if their fingers were on fire. A few of the ladies picked up their skirts, jumped on the raised dance floor, and began an amazing tap dance of sorts. Their feet kicked and shuffled as fast as the musicians could strum.

Ruth clapped her hands with delight, the hectic, happy music lifting her spirits. Beside her, she noticed Noemie rapping her hands on her thighs. Her toes were tapping and the woman's whole body was jittering in time with the delirious chords. Suddenly, and not to Ruth's surprise, Noemie jumped in with the ladies. Their feet thundered on the wood, faster and faster, the banjos and dulcimers filling the air with the raucous, high-pitched, tinny music.

Around her, everyone was smiling, clapping, a few were hooting and hollering, cheering the dancers on. Their skirts were a swirling kaleidoscope of colors. A young boy leaning on a crutch cast it off and joined in the fun, shuffling his feet with the rambunctious rhythm, swinging Noemie around and around.

"Oh, my," Ruth said, laughing, "It reminds me of the dances I went to when I was a child. But we didn't move our arms. We weren't so joyful."

Montgomery was laughing and clapping as well, cheering Noemie on, but he leaned down and asked, "Why didn't you move your arms?"

"Our dance was an expression of resistance to the

English. A reminder we weren't free, but we'd not stop dreaming."

Montgomery nodded his head as if understanding, then he grabbed Ruth's hand. "Welcome to America." He pulled her into the flowing, jittering stream of dancers and commenced kicking his feet and shuffling his toes in rhythm with the music. At first, Ruth resisted, she couldn't remember the steps. Then, as if her feet had minds of their own, she, too, was tapping, shuffling, kicking. She whirled and spun about on Montgomery's arm, then the lad with the crutch took her, spun her, and sent her back to Montgomery.

The joy and the raucous activity nearly stole her breath. She danced and danced and laughed until finally the band, with a few final saws of the bow, ended the song. The crowd cheered its approval. A few folks drifted away from the platform.

Shortly, an older gentleman in a tailored wool suit stepped in front of the musicians and patted the air. The rowdy crowd hesitantly quieted down, expressing their disappointment with a collective groan. Before he opened his mouth, Ruth knew this man must be the senator.

She leaned into Montgomery as the politician began his speech. "I'm sure whatever he has to say," she whispered, "is important, but I'm dyin' of thirst."

She meant to excuse herself, but Montgomery surprised her by taking her elbow, leading her off the dance floor and back to their table. Her arm tingling from his grip, Ruth collapsed gratefully into her chair and all but guzzled her lemonade.

Smacking her lips with satisfaction, she set the glass down and grinned like a fool. "That was the most fun I've had, quite literally in years." Montgomery had a strange look on his face. Ruth couldn't decipher it. Amusement twinkled in his eyes and his lips tipped up in a half-grin. He seemed *tickled* at her, for lack of a better way to word of it. She tilted her head. "Am I entertaining to ye, your lordship?"

Before he could answer, Noemie dropped between them and downed her own glass of lemonade. "By jingles," she said, still a bit winded, "I forgot how much I missed my mountain music." She settled back and sighed. Then her eyes ricocheted back and forth between Montgomery and Ruth. "Am I interrupting something?"

Ruth chuckled. "I think Mr. Boaze was a bit surprised I know how to do something other than work."

His smile grew and he chuckled at them. "Suffice it to say, I'm glad to see both of you having such a fine time."

Noemie glared at the politician over the top of the crowd. "So, how long is that Chee-chalker gonna run his mouth? I wanna dance."

"Ah, go back and tell Jeff Davis we need ammunition, not talk!"

The heckle had come from the group of soldiers who were still passing the bottle around at the back of the beer wagon.

Montgomery's expression darkened. "Senator Neeble is fixing to find out not everyone fighting for the South is fighting for him." He sighed heavily, as if resigned to the trouble the boys heralded.

"Quiet, young man," Senator Neeble growled. "Cap your whiskey and talk to me when you're sober." Most of the crowd chuckled.

"He's got a point," someone in the crowd yelled. "We all know the North's got the munitions. This war drags on, we're gonna be hurtin' for bullets."

Voices murmured angrily in agreement. The four soldiers pushed through the crowd and stepped to the bottom of the stage in front of the senator. "We want the band back. I wanna hear Dixie."

"Yeah, play Dixie," another boy demanded, his words slurring.

Too many inebriated members of the crowd agreed with a loud cheer. Suddenly, the soldiers turned and started thrashing through the crowd. Slowly, Montgomery rose to his feet. Ruth sensed a terrible tension emanating from him.

One of the boys pushed through a group of elderly gentlemen, spied Ruth, and made a beeline for her. Immediately, Montgomery stepped in front of him. He towered over the young man, who glared up at him and took a step back. "Get outta my way, Grandpa. I want a dance with the lady."

Ruth gasped. She could smell the whiskey on the boy from ten feet away. Montgomery placed a hand on the soldier's chest and pushed him back a step. "I'm not sure the young lady wants to dance, son."

The other three soldiers emerged from the crowd. Those standing nearby were following all this turmoil with wide eyes or annoyed expressions. The boys spotted Montgomery forcing their comrade back and hurried to his side.

"Hey, what's going on here?" one asked. The company of drunken soldiers fanned out in a semi-circle around Montgomery.

Her heart leaping into her throat, Ruth surged to her feet. "Montgomery, please." She couldn't bear the thought of him getting jumped by all these boys. "It's all right. He just wants a dance."

"Yeah, me too."

"Me too, ma'am."

"I'm in line, too."

Their drunken, lecherous stares roamed over Ruth. Dancing with them, no matter how distasteful it may be, was better than watching Montgomery get pummeled. There were three men, too many to give her confidence of the right outcome.

"All-all right," she stuttered out. "G-gentlemen."

"I insist, Ruth, that you take your seat."

Montgomery's order, issued with such iron in his tone, confused her. Ruth pleaded with her eyes for Noemie to intervene. The woman stood up and took Ruth's arm. "Ruth, these drunken scalawags have been rude and uncouth. It's best you let Montgomery handle them." She pulled Ruth back down into her seat.

"But there are four of them," she whispered.

Noemie grinned knowingly. "Don't worry. He won't hurt them too bad."

———

MONTGOMERY HAD a moment of missing the quiet, mundane days before Ruth and Noemie had returned to South Carolina. It seemed now that every day was an adventure. If not for Darla's mysterious disappearance, he thought he would have enjoyed the break from routine. He was too old to fight, yet he had done a fine job handling the deserter. Now here he was faced with four drunk *boys*. Almost didn't seem fair.

Well, Lord, if I have to do this, please give me the strength of Samson. "You should turn around and leave the party. Go sleep it off somewhere, son. No hard feelings."

The soldiers' eyes bugged out of their heads. The first one who'd wanted to dance with Ruth inched forward. "Pop, you done bumped your head." He slurred his words and swayed slightly as he spoke. He thumped Montgomery on the chest. "We're gonna dance with that pretty belle."

"You're leaving the party. Walk out on your own, or I'll help you. Your choice."

The boy glanced back at his mates and shook his head as if he couldn't fathom what he'd heard. "You're alone, Pop, and I'm not." The other three soldiers inched forward.

Montgomery grabbed the boy's face and shoved him to the ground as hard and as firmly as he could. The drunken soldier went down easily, his reaction thoroughly muddled by the alcohol. In the instant it took his friends to recover from the shock, Montgomery swung a right hook into one man's jaw with bone- rattling force. Before that boy was even on the ground, Montgomery dove into the third man, picked him up over his shoulders, and tossed his body at the fourth man, mowing him down. Both of them rolled to the feet of the crowd, which gasped collectively.

The first soldier was climbing to his feet when Montgomery grabbed him by his collar and the seat of his pants and tossed him into the two trying to gain their feet again. By now, the young soldier who had tossed aside his crutch to dance limped up, accompanied by an older man Montgomery recognized. Jacob Wheedle from over in Six Mile. The two took up positions beside Montgomery and gave the drunk soldiers challenging stares.

The one young man Montgomery had punched was sitting on the ground, holding his jaw. When Montgomery raised an eyebrow at him, the boy raised his hands in return.

"I'm done, mister. I only got one jaw and I wanna keep it."

Montgomery nodded and strode over to the other three. They shook their heads and waved surrender. Smiling, Montgomery reached out and helped each one to their feet. "Now, you boys go somewhere you can stay out of trouble."

"Glad you don't fight for the Yankees," one of them muttered, turning away.

Wheedle slapped Montgomery on the shoulder. "Sorry my boy and me missed that."

"Speak for yourself, Pa," the soldier said. "I ain't in no hurry for any more fighting."

Montgomery shook their hands with earnest appreciation. "I thank you for coming alongside. If they'd sobered up, they might would have given me a little trouble."

As the boy and his father wandered away, Senator Neeble cleared his throat. No one turned to him. The crowd was still watching Montgomery. The senator tried again. "All right, ladies and gentlemen. Show's over. And I agree with those boys. Let's just dance!" This got the crowd's attention and they cheered and clapped, the fight all but forgotten. Aware he'd lost the fight for the audience, Neeble strode from the stage and marched toward Mayor Fowler.

Flexing a sore hand, Montgomery retook his seat. The expressions on Noemie and Ruth's faces stilled him. His cousin glowed like the proud mother of a spelling bee champion. Ruth looked...she looked...admiring.

"Montgomery, I'm sorry ye got into that fray on my behalf."

Noemie guffawed. "Look at him, girl. He's not even breathing hard."

"Two tussles in a week. Do ye always do this much scrapping?"

Montgomery didn't know the best response here. He was just glad the altercation had been more like a spanking than a fight. He'd read the boys right. They were too drunk and too young to be real trouble. He shrugged and said simply, "No. Just lately it seems I've had something worth fighting for."

He saw a change in Ruth's face, something tender flickered in her eyes, but he couldn't be sure. He'd never be sure. He'd fought to protect her, and he'd do it again. It didn't change the years between them.

The band started up again, this time with a more subdued, weeping fiddle rendition of The Ballad of Fancy Darrow. A moment later, Bear strode up, a plate of apple pie in his hand. "Mr. Boaze, that was some right good fighting. I wish you would teach me sometime."

"Well, I suppose, if it would be all right with your pa."

"Was his idea."

"Oh." That startled Montgomery and he shrugged. "Well, we'll make some time then."

Bear nodded and switched his attention to Noemie and Ruth. "I wouldn't mind a dance with you ladies in a little while."

"That would be lovely," Ruth said.

"You could talk me into it." Noemie winked at him. "If you can keep up."

"I try. Right now," he swiped one last bite from the plate and set it on the table. "I have another young lady I would like to dance with." He beamed from ear to ear. "I will square my shoulders and look her in the eye."

This made no sense to Montgomery, but the news seemed to delight Ruth and Noemie. With a confident nod, the boy turned and walked over to a gaggle of teenage girls. One pretty, petite redhead looked at him with near-boredom as he spoke. She nodded politely, listening with scant attention, but then Bear turned on his heel and marched back over to Montgomery's table.

"What was all that about?" he asked the boy.

"We will see." He winked at Ruth and Noemie, who giggled like schoolgirls.

"She's watching you, lad," Ruth whispered in a conspiratorial tone.

"And I reckon it looks like she's talking about you to her friends," Noemie added.

Montgomery leaned back to observe the three, hiding a wry smile behind his hand, wondering what they were up to.

"Oh," Ruth gasped, clutching his hand. "Don't turn around. She's making her way to our table."

Noemie and Ruth busied themselves, nibbling at a piece of cornbread, taking a sip of the lemonade. The pretty little ginger wandered up behind Bear. Montgomery motioned with a finger. "You've got company."

Bear took a breath, seemed to gather his confidence, and rounded casually on the girl. "Millicent."

"Bjorn, I..." the girl batted her eyelashes at him, "I was wondering if you might like to have some ice cream...with me."

"Well, I..." he dragged out his answer, as if he really couldn't quite decide. "I suppose I could do that." Montgomery's brow rose a little at the boy's surprising confidence. Bear offered the young lady his elbow and the two strolled off into the crowd.

Noemie slapped the table and declared with passion, "I

declare that young man is gonna break hearts in three counties."

Ruth shook her head, laughing. "Oh, what have we done, Noemie? What have we done?"

"Yes, tell me." Montgomery wasn't sure if he should be amused or concerned by this new side to Bear. "What *have* you done?"

Noemie and Ruth exchanged mischievous looks and burst into giddy laughter.

———

LEROY NODDED at the mayor and offered, "Yes," and "That's a fine idea," in the appropriate places, but he was really busy watching those fine, brave, *drunk* Confederate soldiers disappear like scalded dogs. He'd forgotten all about the plate of cold barbecue in his hand, his mind was so busy whirling with possibilities.

"Leroy, you're not listening." Fowler glared at him.

"I heard every word you said. But all that matters is you're saying you want another donation." Leroy skimmed his gaze over the crowd. Some folks were dancing, most were eating and drinking. Everyone was laughing, as if the disturbance with Montgomery and the soldiers had never happened.

"Well, uh," Fowler stumbled. "Yes, I suppose that is the bottom line. I can't make the changes I want in this town if I lose to the merchants and sawmill interests. We farmers need to stick together."

Leroy wondered how long it had been since Fowler steered a plow. Not that it mattered. He was a good boy. He did what he was told. The mayor couldn't help Leroy with his current problem, though. Nor could the young man sitting in jail over Darla's disappearance. Leroy would have never dreamed that would have worked out so well and quickly. He'd known planting the locket had been brilliance.

But it left him with a problem. He was short a man. Perhaps those fine, brave Confederates skedaddling down the road might be of service—if he could sober them up long enough to handle a task.

CHAPTER FOURTEEN

THE GLOW OF THE DANCE STAYED WITH RUTH FOR WEEKS. As life at the farm settled into a pleasant, peaceful routine, it was almost easy to forget the bad things. Montgomery came by often to check on them, dining with them, playing checkers with Bear. Ruth and Bear were attending church now, riding with Montgomery. He made much ado about the fact that he was merely a protector for the ladies, but Ruth had her moments when she wondered about his true intentions. She wondered about her own.

There weren't many young men in Oconee County because of the war, and the few she'd met both at the dance that night and in church didn't impact her in the least. But Montgomery did. She delighted in his company more and more with every visit. Her heart sang when he sparred playfully with Noemie, ruffled Bear's hair after a good game, or sat down beside her in the pew. She wasn't sure what her heart was telling her, but she knew one thing: she was happy here.

So happy, she had to remind herself often to temper her good moods in front of Noemie.

Weeding the kitchen garden, Ruth paused to wipe sweat from her forehead and consider her mother-in-law for a moment. Sitting in the shade, shelling peas, she looked content. Their lives were coming back together, healing, but Noemie had lost so much. She rarely let her pain show, but Ruth had heard Noemie walking the floors at night. Even heard her once in the wee, quiet hours, scolding the Lord for being so hardhearted toward her.

These conversations grieved Ruth, and she attempted to counter them with her own prayers. *Lord, please help Noemie find her love for You again. Lord, please help her forgive You, even though You didn't take her son or her husband.*

"Stop staring at me, 'less you got something you want to say."

Ruth blinked and went back to weeding. "No, I was just thinking..." She paused, decided to risk a statement that might hurt Noemie, but put it out there anyway. "I'm happy here, Noemie. In fact, I love it here. This is the happiest I've ever been in my whole life. I'm sorry if that hurts ye."

Noemie's hand stilled as she seemed to consider the statement. "Some wounds never heal, Ruth, but you come to terms with them. You're happy? That truly makes me happy. And, honestly..." She sighed and looked out over the farm. "I'm adjusting. Life goes on."

"Knock, knock."

Both women started at the voice and the thumping sound. They looked up as Pastor Kenneth lowered his hand from the side of the house.

"Morning, Kenneth," Noemie greeted.

"Noemie. Ruth."

"Out visiting the flock today, are ye, Reverend?"

"Well, uh, yes and no."

He tugged at his collar as if he were a bit nervous and Ruth wondered what in the world he could be here to see her about.

"I was wondering if I might sit a spell with Noemie. She won't come to church...and I'd like..." His face softened as he gazed at her. Ruth had to stop her mouth from falling open. "I'd just like to visit, if you've time, Noemie."

Ruth surged to her feet. "I'll bring ye some lemonade." *Thank the Lord for lemonade.*

"Ain't none."

"I'll make it." She rushed past the reverend. "You two go sit by the pond. I'll bring yer drinks shortly."

––––––––

NOEMIE BLINKED STUPIDLY AT KENNETH. Ruth's sudden departure bewildered her. Why had the girl acted like her tail was on fire? Noemie set her bowl aside and stood. "I always have time for you, Kenneth." And she did. She had always enjoyed his company, and if not for Luke coming along, perhaps their friendship would have gone in a different direction.

All water under the bridge now, she thought, as they ambled down to the pond. "How are things in the church, Kenneth?"

He shrugged. "God is still on the throne. Jesus still forgives sins."

"That is good to know." Noemie considered this religious small talk, but she knew that for Kenneth, it was likely more. They settled on the bench in the shade of a willow tree and watched a school of rainbow trout soar and glide through the water. "Bear built it this summer. Dug it out. Dammed the creek. Now, anytime we want fried trout…"

Kenneth looked impressed. "He's not an idle lad, is he?"

"No. Between him and Ruth, we'll have this place on its feet by next harvest."

"I noticed your corn on the way in. Despite the dry weather, it's the best looking in the valley."

"Good soil down by the river. We'll start harvesting Friday. Montgomery, bless his heart, is loaning us some men."

"He's a good neighbor."

"Yes, he is. He sold me some fine cattle and they're all fat and sassy now. I tell you, it's cost me nearly everything to get this place fixed up, but we're going to have a good harvest, financially speaking."

"Praise God."

"If you say so."

Kenneth's shoulders sagged. "Ruth told me you're holding a grudge against God."

"More like He's holding a grudge against me."

Kenneth leaned forward, rested his elbows on his knees, and tapped his fingertips together. "I didn't really come to talk about spiritual issues, but I will say this. God's not the enemy. If you are holding a grudge, Noemie "— he looked over his shoulder at her— "you've got it aimed in the wrong direction."

His eyes, the color of her morning coffee, had always comforted Noemie, reflecting an enduring friendship that she treasured. She exhaled a long, deep breath and nodded. "Maybe so. It's just hard to think when you're so tangled up in pain and anger."

Kenneth bit his bottom lip and nodded but didn't say anything else.

Noemie appreciated him not beating her over the head with a sermon. He seemed to understand she needed time. Finally, she asked, "What *did* you come by to talk about?" The rhythm of his tapping fingers jumped noticeably, and his foot started twitching like he had an ant in his shoe. "What's the matter with you? If you've got some bad news, just spit it out. I'm pretty sure I can bear it."

He shook his head and smiled at her. "I'm out of practice." He straightened up, brushed some hair off his forehead, and looked her in the eye. "Would you let me take you to dinner, Noemie?"

She heard the words, but for the life of her couldn't make sense of what he was asking. "What?"

"Dinner, as in allow me to escort you to a restaurant for a formal—that is to say, I'm asking officially if I might...court you." Noemie's mouth literally fell open. Kenneth winced. "That's not the reaction I was hoping for."

"Well, what did you expect? I thought you'd come to talk to me about salvation, or that you needed a donation for the church." She slumped against the bench, overwhelmed. "I don't know, Kenneth."

He pinched sweat from his lip and fluttered his lips. "I was kind of hoping I might have been on your mind some. Guess you've had a lot to contend with, though. It's just that, ever since you came back into the valley, I've been thinking about you. I saw you at the Fourth of July barbecue and you looked and acted so much like the girl I remember."

"You didn't even speak to me at the barbecue."

"You noticed?"

"Yeah, and I was almost offended. Why didn't you at least say howdy?"

"Because…" He chuckled, ran his tongue over his teeth. "I wanted to see if you'd stick with me."

"I don't understand."

"I wasn't going to ask you to dinner or even for a coffee unless I knew for sure this was no crush. At my age—our age—we don't have time to waste on trivial pursuits."

Noemie almost gave him an amen to that. She folded her arms and considered things for a moment. Maybe dinner would be a way to find out if *he'd* stick with *her*. But what if he did? "All right. I ain't making you any promises, though." The screen door slammed and she looked across the backyard at Ruth carrying two drinks in her hands. "I've got a lot of things to consider, Kenneth. *My* happiness ain't at the top of the list."

———

RUTH STARED at her reflection in her vanity mirror and brushed out her long locks, auburn and caramel highlights reflecting the lamplight. Her mind, though, was on the picture of Noemie riding off this evening with the reverend. The image made the grin on her face spread. What a precious couple they made. And then to find out— through a hesitant confession from Noemie—they'd actually been a couple many, many years ago. And she seemed to have enjoyed her evening with him, though she hadn't been eager to share details. Yet.

"Oh, wouldn't it be lovely, Lord," she whispered, "if You blessed her latter end, like Job, more than her beginning? I would wish that for her."

Rain drops intermittently sounded on the tin roof over

her head, and lightning rumbled from somewhere up in the mountains. A cool breeze wafted in the window, carrying the moist scent of grass and earth. In quick order, though, the rain picked up and she was forced to close it.

The sound on the roof, however, was soothing, and she smiled to herself as she turned out her lamp and crawled into freshly laundered sheets. Sleep claimed her before she could finish saying good night to the Lord.

———

A FEROCIOUS, booming rumble of thunder exploded over the farm, rattling Ruth's window. She sat bolt upright in the bed as lightning flashed, illuminating the room. Rain beat hard against the window.

Just a storm...

But a wiggle of fear slithered up her spine.

A gun shot—no, more thunder—boomed and rolled over the house as lightning streaked across the sky. But she also heard—or felt—an underlying sound, *like* thunder but long and steady, growing louder. Muddled by sleep but perplexed, she rose and went to her window to watch the light show. Lightning streaked across the sky...and illuminated a chilling scene below. She gasped in horror.

The cattle were stampeding across the hill, headed toward the house.

Her heart hammered like a cannonade in her chest. For an instant, she thought she saw a flash of blond hair disappear behind the barn.

Bear?

Terrified, Ruth ran from her room screaming for Noemie...

CHAPTER FIFTEEN

THERE WAS NOTHING THEY COULD DO. A RIVER OF TWO hundred cattle, close-packed and wild-eyed, was roaring from the back of the house, surging across the kitchen garden, flowing in front of the house, down the hill, and beginning to tear into the corn. Though the cacophony of thunder, driving rain, and hundreds of hooves was deafening, Ruth screamed for Bear from the porch. Her voice disappeared into the swirling mass of the storm and bawling animals.

Noemie emerged from the house with her shotgun and fired it over the cattle, but they were all one solid mass of mindless, panicked flesh. They couldn't hear. They couldn't see. They could only run from the thunder overhead. She pulled the second trigger back and moved down to the top step. She fired again, but she might as well have been blowing a flute for all the reaction she got from the herd.

Ruth reached out and pulled her back up on the porch. "There's nothing we can do but pray." She prayed Bear was safe, she prayed there'd be something left of the crops...

She prayed for daylight.

————

WHEN DAYLIGHT CAME, the destruction took Ruth's breath away. She and Noemie stared in dismal shock at the once lush, green kitchen garden that now resembled a muddy hog wallow. The herd had left a swampy, shredded trail of earth from the back pasture, around the house, and across the front yard. They'd swarmed over the coop, leveling it and scattering lumber. A few traumatized chickens walked about in a daze or sat on the corral fence, fluffing their feathers.

Then the herd had turned down the hill and run straight for the corn and tobacco. Not only had they trampled the crops into the ground, scores of them milled about in it now, munching on the green ears. Ruth shook her head and commanded her legs to hold her upright. Her heart was in her throat, but she prayed for the strength not to weep in defeat in front of Noemie.

Noemie surveyed the destruction with a pained crease in her forehead and tight, thin lips. Yet, she uttered not a word, other than to call for Bear as they walked. Ruth was sick to her stomach with fear. The devastation was awful, but the boy—where was he? *Oh, God, let him be all right...*

They stopped on the hill overlooking the once beautiful, twelve-foot-high corn, now reduced to a muddy, garbled mess. "Did you hear gunshots last night?"

"No. Maybe." Ruth shook her head. "I'm not sure. For a moment, I thought I did."

Noemie raised her chin and squared her shoulders. "Let's saddle up the horses. We need to find Bear."

THE STILLNESS after a rain was something Montgomery had always appreciated. He and Lucy trotted along the trail to Noemie's, enjoying the late summer air this morning and stunning blue sky overhead. The trail ended in Noemie's northernmost pasture. Instead of unlocking the gate for his horse, Montgomery let Lucy jump it. Encouraged by her energy, he started to kick her up to a gallop, but suddenly pulled her to a stop instead. Something was wrong.

He noticed the silence first.

Then he realized the cattle that usually milled around here were gone.

Nothing to worry about, really. The whole herd could have moved to the other side of the ridge. A finger of unease poked at him, though, and he nudged Lucille up to a lope and they headed in toward the house. Moments later, he emerged from a draw on the backside of the house and immediately saw the wide, dark path of wildly churned up soil. He followed it, took in the destroyed garden with concern, and hurried around to the front.

The chicken coop looked as if a twister had hit it. Flat as a flapjack, parts of it had been scattered in a line with the path of devastation. He was trying to digest what he was seeing when Noemie and Ruth emerged from the barn on horseback. They saw him and trotted over.

"We need some help, Montgomery."

Those words out of Noemie's mouth spoke volumes. "Anything. What happened here?"

"I think somebody stampeded the cattle. Tore up everything, but what matters is we can't find Bear."

Montgomery tried to ignore the sinking in his gut. "All right. Where do we start?"

"We've looked close to the house…" Ruth began.

"Now we've gotta search the fields," Noemie finished somberly for her.

They agreed to split up and search separately, knowing it would be a faster way to cover ground. Ruth had said she thought she'd seen Bear disappear behind the barn, so Montgomery took the land west and north of the house. Ruth went south, and Noemie east. They agreed to meet at the house at noon.

The cattle had stampeded across the farm, going from southeast to northwest, a long, dark scar shooting across Noemie's place at an angle. Thanking God that at least she and Ruth were safe, he searched the destroyed corn and tobacco fields carefully. He circled around the perimeter of the largest section and was about to turn back when he saw a flash of white—no, yellow—showing in the trampled corn.

The twisted, bloody, half-buried body in the mud hit him like a mule's kick.

CHAPTER SIXTEEN

BARELY ABLE TO SEE THROUGH HER TEARS, RUTH WASHED Bear's body as she listened to Montgomery and Noemie discuss the stampede in the parlor. They'd laid the boy out on a table in the laundry room, stripped him except for a sheet across his midsection, and then Ruth had asked Montgomery to go sit with Noemie. She couldn't believe the young boy before her wouldn't ever open his eyes again and ask for more flapjacks.

"What do you think you heard?" Montgomery asked softly in the other room.

"I heard rifle shots. I'm sure of it." Noemie's voice cracked with audible rage. "They didn't stampede. They were stampeded."

"There was a big storm last night," he said. "Thunder and lightning could have caused it."

"Bear was outside with his gun. You found it by his side. He was after somebody—" Her voice broke. "Why does God keep doing this to me?"

"God didn't do this, Noemie." Montgomery's tone changed, and it made the hair on her neck stand up. "But if this was no accident, God help whoever did."

Why, Ruth wondered, as she washed the mud and blood away from Bear's face. *Why? Who did this to you?* His vivid blue eyes, so full of life, stared blankly at nothing. Their emptiness, so final and cold, worked a sob from her. Once his face and hair were washed, she laid coins upon his eyelids, unable to bear the lifeless gaze. "I'm sorry, Bear. So sorry."

Ruth dropped a sponge full of water on the boy's chest and gasped as the mud and blood washed away. "Montgomery, come here!"

He bounded around the corner, froze when he saw her face. "What is it?"

She pointed at Bear's chest.

The bullet hole was unmistakable.

————

MONTGOMERY SAT DOWN HARD in the Empire-style chair and stared across the parlor at Noemie. After a moment, he squeezed his eyes shut and tried to think, to sort the maelstrom of thoughts and emotions whirling in his brain into something that made sense. First and foremost, he accepted the soul-jarring relief he felt knowing Ruth was safe. But he had to think beyond that, deal with it later. Noemie was safe, thank God, but the stinging grief over Bear's death tried to drag his thoughts to a crawl.

Stop it, Montgomery, he scolded. *The boy's dead. Nothing can be done for him.* But Ruth and Noemie—he wouldn't be able to stand it if anything happened to either of them.

"You and Ruth, pack a few things and go to my house."

Noemie frowned and opened her mouth, but he raised a hand cutting her off. "Noemie, please. I have enough to worry about. Maybe it was deserters who did this. Maybe it was Leroy. Maybe Bear's death was an accident. But until I know for sure, I need you where I can protect you."

"A hole in his chest is no accident."

"I know," he said with resignation.

Ruth stepped into the room and stood behind the chair Noemie occupied. Her cheeks were flushed, and a few hairs flew loose from her braid. "Bear's ready." She squeezed Noemie's shoulder. "And we'll be ready in five minutes."

Montgomery waited for their footfalls to fade on the stairs and then went to retrieve Bear. Ruth had wrapped him lovingly in a quilt and secured him with rope. Montgomery patted the boy's foot and swallowed the knot in his throat. "I'll find out what happened, Bear. God as my witness, they won't get away with it."

"Noemie?"

"I'm out here, Montgomery, admiring the view." Noemie didn't really want any company, but it was his house, not hers. She had decided, however, that she liked his porch swing right much and thought she might buy one—

She stopped the thought. After this, she wasn't going to have enough money to buy so much as a candle, much less something as frivolous as a porch swing. Least not till they got the cattle to market, and that would barely be enough to cover the bills. There would be very little extra.

In the meantime, they were pretty dang broke. She

could claim a little pocket change that wouldn't be enough to buy a week's food. Unless they wanted to live off Montgomery, and the thought of charity turned her stomach.

They'd worked so hard. Now they were nearly broke, and Bear was dead. It all seemed so hopeless. She didn't know if she should scream with rage or grief first.

Her tall, handsome cousin stepped out on the back porch and scanned the farm, the hills, and pastures beyond with a weary posture. The sun had gone down behind the mountains, setting the sky ablaze.

Another day done, Noemie thought. *Another tragedy. Another example of Your hand against me, Lord.* She felt like shaking her fist at heaven but clenched her jaws instead.

Montgomery shoved his hands in his pockets and sighed. "I went back over to your place looking for clues. The rain washed everything away. We did get your cattle rounded back up and put in the north pasture."

"Thank you, cousin. I appreciate it." And she did, but she also hated this necessary dependency on him.

He acknowledged the courtesy with a little nod and then sat down in a chair made of bent willow, his shoulders rounded, his countenance weary. A sigh escaped him.

"I told you once you didn't take us to raise. Looks like maybe I was wrong."

He waved away her concerns. "You're my family and you're in need. Don't let pride enter into this, Noemie. I want you safe. More than anything, that's what I want."

"Losing the crops was a blow. I was counting on that as extra money. Thanks for helping with the cattle, though."

"There's always next year. For now, you're my guests. Don't worry about anything."

"You know I can't accept charity. I won't accept it."

Montgomery tilted his head, studying Noemie.

She could read his mind. "I know I'm prideful. You'll just have to accept it."

He mulled things over for a moment, studying her the whole time. "All right. How about this? Glean the fields. Take what you get and can it, store it in my root cellar, whatever you need. In return, help me around the house."

Ruth stepped outside just then, smiled at Noemie, and patted Montgomery on the shoulder. "That's a generous offer. Don't you think, Noemie?"

She narrowed her eyes at him. "Yeah, but just how long do you figure to keep us here?"

"You make it sound like I've arrested you."

"I know you're trying to help, Montgomery, and I know you worry over us. Bear's death is a heartbreaking, frightening thing. But I tell you right now, I'm not staying away from my home for long."

He patted the air. "Just a few days. Maybe a week. Or two. We need to figure out who was behind the stampede, and then we'll know what happened to Bear."

A troubled dip in her brow, Ruth drifted by him and joined Noemie on the swing. "The hog dying—"

"Getting butchered," Noemie corrected.

"Butchered," she corrected. "And Darla disappearing. Then Bear shot dead, our cattle stampeded."

"You think it's all related?" Montgomery asked.

"Don't you?"

"Yes, but I don't know how or why. Or, most importantly, who."

"I suspect Mr. Heyward," Ruth said firmly.

"Based on what?" Montgomery asked.

"Based on the fact that I don't like him."

Noemie considered the complaint, but it didn't

convince her. "He's no saint. In fact, he's a real pain in the rear, but murder?"

"Maybe Bear's death was not intentional, but you have to ask, if someone stampeded your cattle, why?" Ruth asked.

"I thought about that." Noemie had a suspicion that made a lot of sense in her mind. "What if it was deserters? Maybe they stampeded the cattle as a diversion, so they could steal a few head."

"And Bear stumbled on them?" Ruth asked.

"That's what I think." She also thought she'd go home to her damaged farm as soon as she could. This living off Montgomery didn't taste right. She glanced between him and Ruth and the chemistry there pained her some. Still, time together might be best for *them*.

Not for her, though. She'd come home to live on the old home place. If it hadn't been for Ruth's insistence, she'd be there now, sitting on her front porch with a shotgun across her lap. But she'd give Montgomery a little time to sort things out.

And gleaning his field in exchange for some cleaning was acceptable to her pride.

———

RUTH AND NOEMIE hit the fields bright and early to glean. Mercifully, the day was overcast, the humidity low, and the work not as hard as it could have been for a late August day. Ruth couldn't understand why they were the only hands out digging sweet potatoes, aside from a few of Montgomery's men.

"If we're gleaning," Noemie said, dropping her hoe in the ground, "where is everybody else?"

"I was wondering the same thing."

A little while later, Billy Rafferty, Montgomery's foreman, rolled by with a water wagon and stopped. "You ladies like a sip?" He jumped down without waiting for an answer and grabbed the ladle hanging from the keg. The women stopped their work and obliged themselves, Ruth tossing a sweet potato in her basket as she walked by it.

Noemie guzzled a good, full ladle and returned to work, but Ruth dallied over her water for a moment, making sure her mother-in-law was out of range. "Mr. Rafferty, I want to ask ye something."

Rafferty was a kind- looking man with gray hair and a tanned, leathery face. A farmer all his life, Ruth suspected. He nodded and said, "Shoot."

"Why are we gleaning these fields? Clearly Montgomery hasn't opened them to the community yet. I've seen yer own men out here still."

"Maybe it's a gift. Why don't you accept it graciously?"

"A gift or charity?" Ruth had worked hard all her life and never once accepted a handout. The notion had never sat well with her.

Rafferty cut his eyes at Noemie, then back to Ruth. "Don't she need taking care of? It'd be a fool thing to let your pride make her hungry, too."

Ruth was humbled by the man's wise words. She'd only been thinking of herself. She handed him the ladle. "Thank you for your correction, Mr. Rafferty."

He winked at her. "You're welcome."

By evening, Ruth and Noemie had harvested several baskets of sweet potatoes, corn, peas, and squash. Some things they would can, some Noemie insisted they would store in the root cellar at her place sometime in the next few days. Tomorrow, Mr. Rafferty said they could harvest the onions and some carrots, as well as go through the cabbage fields.

They tried to gather only what would get them through to next spring, well aware that other folks in Oconee County would have need as well. And they went to bed grateful that night for a kinsman redeemer.

CHAPTER SEVENTEEN

AN UNEXPECTED NIP IN THE MORNING AIR REMINDED Montgomery that fall was nigh. Glad for it, he snapped the reins and drove the wagon off to the cabbage fields. It had taken a great amount of mental discipline and plenty of prayers to get his focus back on the reality of things— namely, accepting his age and hers—and now with the woman beside him, he felt that discipline slipping. He couldn't begin to explain why she made his heart race or his knees weak, especially when she turned those simmering, warm brown eyes on him, but he had to stop this nonsense.

She was safe. He'd keep her safe. Eventually, they'd get to the source of this trouble and she and Noemie could go home. And he'd try with everything in him to help them, but he had to distance himself from her. He glanced over at her and felt the bite of regret. He regretted the gap between them and wished he were a decade younger.

"What is it, Montgomery?" she asked softly. "You look a little sad. Is it Bear?"

He was no child, and therefore did not feel the need to lie, though he worded his answer carefully. "I was thinking how relieved I am that you and Noemie are safe. I'm truly sorry about Bear, but for all we know, he died saving your lives."

She studied him for a moment, and he wished he could read her mind. "I slept well last night. I feel safe here, but Noemie won't stay long."

Which meant Ruth would go with her.

He cleared his throat and stared hard at the dirt road in front of them. "I know." He had to get to the bottom of all this trouble. Obviously, the stampede had not been an accident. In fact, Montgomery saw it as a warning. A warning that was getting louder, but Noemie wasn't listening. This was all conjecture, but what if he was right?

"Ruth, I have an idea I want to run by you." He lowered his voice so Noemie, sitting on the tail-end of the wagon, couldn't hear.

"All right. Shoot." She smiled.

"For years, Leroy told folks he bought Noemie's farm outright. When she got here, though, he backtracked fast, didn't want us poking around the deed office, and moved his cattle off in a big hurry."

"Aye, all true so far."

"What if he's behind all of this trouble and he's doing it to scare you two off?"

"She won't scare. Not even after Bear's death. I can see it in her eyes. Ye don't know the trouble I had getting her here."

"No, I do know." Short of being hog-tied, Noemie wouldn't stay put for long. "I'd like to choke Leroy to within an inch of his life, but I don't have any proof of anything. The sheriff can't do a dang thing to him, either. All he can do is *look into things.*"

Ruth squeezed his shoulder. "Ye'll figure something out."

He looked down at her. Her expression was kind and trusting. Wide, bright eyes filled with admiration pulled the focus right out from under him again. Was he reading her wrong? She almost looked as if she wanted a kiss.

It didn't matter. No dreamy gaze changed anything, didn't make him twenty-five again. He'd promised himself she wouldn't wind up like him, stuck, alone, hiding from the world. He snapped his attention back to the road ahead. "I'll do my best. Maybe tomorrow after the funeral I can ask some questions, too."

———

RUTH TOOK a seat on the bench in front of Fowler's Mercantile and waited for Noemie. Sweat trickled down her back, between her breasts. A humid day, she wiped moisture off her forehead with the back of her hand. Late summer was, she admitted, a touch more tolerable in Maryland. The early morning heat here had added another depressing element to an already solemn day. She brushed lint off her black skirt and sighed, recalling James's warm smiles and Bear's shy laughter—nothing left of them now but memories. Thin, fragile memories.

A moment later, a screen door banged and Noemie stepped outside the store. "Here. You can probably use this."

Her expression somber, she handed Ruth the root beer and sat down beside her. "Heck of a thing, a funeral for a young man cut down in the prime of his life."

Ruth wondered if Noemie was referring to Bear's life or James's. Not that it mattered. The statement was still true. "His mother looked shattered. I felt terrible for her. As I do still for you."

Noemie wiggled her nose and sniffed, as if trying to stop tears. "You don't get over it. You just sort of…get used to the pain. You start out crying at the drop of a hat, and then you gradually get a little more control, but it ain't *healing* exactly. Just…control."

Ruth took a sip from the bottle and didn't say anything. James's death was terrible, but she couldn't pretend a grief she didn't feel. Bear's death hurt more. After a few minutes, she tried to get their minds off the dead. "I wonder how much longer Montgomery will be."

"Probably isn't far behind us. He knew Bear's parents, but not real well. I doubt he'll do more than make a respectable appearance."

Sure enough, he rolled up a moment later in the wagon. "You ladies good? Ready to head back?"

They climbed up into the wagon, Ruth putting no thought into where she sat, but she wound up in the front with Montgomery, Noemie in the back seat. They rode along in a sad, brooding silence until he broke it. "I ran into Heyward."

Noemie's head snapped up. "And?"

"He denied any involvement with Bear's death. Denied it vehemently."

Noemie crossed her arms and scowled at the world. "We need to find out who did this."

"The sheriff went by Tunnel Hill. Leroy and his vigilance committee insisted on going with him. They skirmished with some boys up there, but they skedaddled. The sheriff didn't catch anybody, didn't see any cattle, either."

"What's Tunnel Hill?" Ruth asked.

"About nine, ten years ago, the South Carolina legislature funded a railroad project. The line was supposed to go from Charleston to the Ohio Valley. Because of the war, though, they killed the project. There are still some cabins up there and a tunnel in the mountain. Deserters try to hide in them occasionally."

"The boys Sheriff Holden tussled with," Noemie began, "any chance they stampeded the cattle?"

"The sheriff thinks they were the responsible parties."

"But he didn't catch anybody," she said, obviously disgusted.

"I'm going to talk to him again about it, when Leroy's not around. He was hovering the whole time, acting like he wasn't listening."

"Is Holden looking for those deserters? Bear's got to have some justice, Montgomery."

He looked over his shoulder at his cousin and nodded. "I want that, too. Sheriff Holden and his deputies have been out looking. Somehow, those boys got hold of some horses and lit a shuck out. The posse followed, but the trail petered out."

Noemie huffed and settled back but didn't say anything else. For her part, Ruth had listened and prayed for justice for Bear and comfort for his poor mother.

"Noemie, Ruth, I hope y'all won't mind..." Montgomery cleared his throat. "Well, I invited a guest for dinner. Vincent Jack. He's home recovering from a lead ball to his thigh. Won't be here much longer." He cast a quick, nervous glance over at Ruth. "I thought you might enjoy meeting him, Ruth. He's a good man. I've known him since he was ten."

Ruth felt her face freeze like a mask of ice and was sure

her expression was a mix of shock and indignation...and hurt. She quickly looked out at the buildings as they rode out of town. Anger flared in her chest at Montgomery's audacity.

"I didn't mean, I mean, I—I didn't say anything about you in a particular way as to set any expectations. I just said you and Noemie would be there." He faltered, as if expecting her to say something, but she bit her tongue and held her peace. And kept her gaze off him.

"Is that Charlie's boy?" Noemie asked.

"Yes, ma'am."

"Yeah, I reckon he would be around Ruth's age. He'd just turned nineteen or so when James and me left for Maryland. I always liked him. Never had a bad word for anybody."

"Except Yankees. They took out half his unit."

"Vile war," Noemie spat.

Still, Ruth kept her silence. She was afraid that if she spoke, she might go off on these two like a stick of dynamite.

———

RUTH HAD no time to gather her thoughts before she and Noemie had to head into the kitchen and start dinner. She was curt and clipped in her conversation with the woman, and it didn't take her mother-in-law long to figure out the problem.

"You're mad because he invited a young man over here to meet you, aren't you?"

"Of course, I'm mad." Ruth slammed a rolling pin down on the counter, fortunately not into the center of the biscuits she'd just rolled out. "What's the matter with the man, trying to play matchmaker? I don't need anyone's help to find a husband. I don't want a husband at all. James hasn't even been gone six months." She huffed, blowing a strand of hair from her face. She didn't want a husband, did she? Or was it that she didn't like Montgomery pawning her off on someone else? "And you," she pointed the pin at Noemie. "Talking about things as if we're shopping for a new stove."

Noemie sliced potatoes, casually dropping the pieces into a pot of boiling water as she went. "Don't have a hissy fit with me, little girl. I was just making an observation about the man, in case the idea tickled your fancy."

Ruth fussed and fumed for a moment, then finally nodded as she slipped biscuits into the oven. "I'm sorry. I was taken aback by Montgomery's interference."

Noemie grunted. "Have to admit, I'm a little puzzled myself. Maybe we're reading too much into it. Maybe he just happened to invite Vincent out here and we—you—were an afterthought, a way to sweeten the invite."

Somehow, Ruth didn't think so. To her, this felt like Montgomery was throwing up a barrier. A shield. Of protection? But whose heart was he guarding?

———

RUTH WAS polite at dinner to Mr. Vincent Jack, but she had no doubt he knew she was not interested. Her answers were soft but clipped and close-ended. And she did not pursue conversation, allowing Montgomery and Noemie to cover the gaps. Eventually, to ease the tension—of which she assumed Mr. Jack was unaware—Montgomery took the man out to the porch to smoke cigars, and a little while later their guest drove off.

Ruth was a touch embarrassed, as she knew she could have been kinder, feigned some interest in the man. After all, he was a soldier, but all she could think about was how to get away from the table and be alone. She felt... discarded by Montgomery, and it hurt her more than she would have expected.

She helped Noemie with the dishes and then excused herself to go for a walk. Montgomery's property had lovely views like Noemie's, but one in particular called to her.

She stopped and stared out over a hayfield golden with wheat ready to cut. One by one, as twilight settled, the lightning bugs came to life, rising up out of the grass. They blinked, floated, meandered i n the summer air. They were almost like conductors, she thought, for the orchestra of crickets.

"Ruth?"

She didn't move, didn't turn to him. How could she explain how she felt? Especially since he didn't feel the same way. She crossed her arms and held her silence.

"Vincent said to give you his regards. I, uh, I am a little concerned...or confused is a better word, I guess." He spoke haltingly. She could hear the uncertainty in his voice. "You didn't seem yourself tonight." She heard him sigh. "Noemie said you—you and she—thought I invited Vincent out here to—that I was playing matchmaker. I won't lie. I was only thinking—"

"No, ye weren't." She whirled. "Not at all. At least not about anyone other than yerself."

"What?" The confusion in his weathered, handsome face would have been comical if Ruth hadn't been so angry with him.

"Ye needn't play games. Ye're quite safe from me, Mr.

Boaze. I've no interest in ye. Please don't presume to play matchmaker again."

"But I...I—" He raised his hand to her. "I don't...I don't...What?"

Ruth raised an eyebrow at him, disgusted with herself for being this emotional and him for being so...stupidly male. " Good night."

She stomped by him. With every step, her heart's pounding grew louder and more jarring. She hoped he'd stop her, call her name, say something...something like...

You're wrong, Ruth. I do care.

But every step away from him in silence nailed home the truth.

CHAPTER EIGHTEEN

THE NEXT MORNING, NOEMIE AGREED TO STAY OUT OF THE field and do some housework for Montgomery. Over the breakfast table, he asked Ruth, "Would you mind gleaning with the Daggerhardts and Kochs? They're two widows with their children."

"Of course not," she said stiffly.

"And Billy said something about a group of men came by yesterday. They're with a foraging unit attached to the 26th out of North Carolina. I'd say stay away from them."

"All right."

He wiped his chin and put down his napkin. "Noemie, thank you for stepping in for Darla."

A sad, awkward silence followed his words. Noemie pursed her lips and nodded. "You're doing us a kindness. I can return the favor."

"Quit beating that horse. You're safe. That's all that matters." He stood and pushed his chair in. "Ruth, I can give you a ride out to the cabbage fields, if you like."

"All right."

Her cold tone was hard to miss, and Montgomery shot Noemie a confused look. She pretended not to see it.

———

NOEMIE HUNG the last of Montgomery's laundry on the line and picked up the empty basket. The man wasn't much to keep up after, being pretty neat on his own. A hawk called from overhead, sailing toward the mountain between here and her place. The peak, beginning to hint at coming fall colors, had been taunting her all morning.

She drummed her fingers on her thigh, debating. No reason she couldn't go home and check on things, of course. It was her place. Billy Rafferty had been making the trip daily himself, but, again, it was *her* place. *Her* home.

Whoever was intent on causing her trouble had been doing so at night. Like most slimy things, the sun scared them off, so a trip in the middle of the day couldn't be safer. Besides, she needed to make sure the root cellar was in good shape to store the food she and Ruth had gleaned. She could maybe tidy up the kitchen garden, as well, see if anything was salvageable.

There were a few things in Bear's room she thought his family ought to have.

That decided it for her. Ten minutes later, she and a palomino mare named Buttercup were loping across Montgomery's pasture, headed for the trail.

———

RUTH WAS NO FOOL. As she slashed a knife through a cabbage stalk, she pondered Montgomery's expression in the wagon over and over. He had looked at her with open longing, but what held him back from saying anything? And why had he thrown another man at her? Her confusion over the look in his eyes melted her anger with him. He seemed to be wrestling with something, perhaps whatever the barrier was between them.

Without her anger, the desire for something more with Montgomery was stark and jarring.

She worked quietly as the other two ladies, Helga and Svenna, jabbered happily in German, slicing off heads of cabbage and tossing them into waiting boxes. Every once in a while, they would look at Ruth, smile politely as if apologizing that she couldn't participate in their conversation, and go right back to jabbering.

Around them, the children ran and played tag, running up and down the rows, jumping across them, but as the day warmed, they fell into playing or napping along the edge of the field in the shade. At lunch time, instead of Billy Rafferty bringing the water wagon, Montgomery rode out with a keg of water, a batch of sandwiches, and bottles of root beer.

Ruth smiled at his generosity as he passed out the food, including candy for the children. "Where did ye get all this?" she asked, grabbing the ladle and getting a drink of water.

"I made a trip into town. I suppose Noemie could have whipped up something, but this was easier." He handed her a sandwich wrapped in waxed paper and a bottle of warm root beer. Their eyes and their fingers met, and Ruth felt a tingle that sizzled up her whole arm. He paused, held her gaze, his look seemed rife with desire. How could she know for sure? Did she want to?

He turned away and handed some licorice to a little

blonde-haired pixie. "There you go, Greta." He patted her on the head and the child skipped off, full of joy.

The group of soldiers walked up then, well-mannered enough to wait until the widows and little ones had been fed, but they barely looked at Montgomery as they queued up for food. All four pairs of eyes roamed boldly over Ruth. Uncomfortable with their brazen stares, she slid to the end of the wagon.

Montgomery, clearly annoyed with them, snapped his fingers in their faces. "Right here, boys. Eyes on me. Mind your manners."

A few of the soldiers scowled at the high-handed scolding but didn't say anything. All of them took their sandwiches and their root beer and drifted off into the shade.

"Thank you." Ruth appreciated his chivalry. In fact, she appreciated just about everything related to Montgomery Boaze. What she wouldn't give if he could read her mind, or, at the very least, her eyes. Surely, they said everything he needed to know. It struck her that possibly that was the problem. Was she *too* obvious? Did it make *her* seem brazen?

Suddenly, he straightened a touch more and raised his chin. "Ruth, would you take a stroll in the shade with me?"

Her back stiffened and she raised her chin. Her initial thought was to give him a sharp *no thank you* because she should still be angry with him over the invitation to Vincent Jack. In truth, however, that was the opposite of what she wanted to say. She softened and nodded. "Aye."

———

HUNDREDS of sharp hooves had absolutely pulverized the kitchen garden, turned the fence into what looked like the debris from a shipwreck, and leveled the chicken coop. A handful of the hardy chickens that survived scratched and pecked around the garden, heedless of the destruction surrounding them.

Sighing, Noemie led Buttercup around to the front of the house and drew up. A sorrel stood quietly in the shade, tied to the hitching post. Not Billy Rafferty's horse. "Now, who the heck...?"

She trailed off and listened for a moment. She thought she heard the faint sound of someone moving about in the house. She wrapped Buttercup's reins around a tree branch and crept up to the front door.

Yes, from inside she heard what sounded like desk drawers opening and closing. Noemie pulled the screen door open slowly, pausing before the point where it usually creaked, and slipped inside.

She soft-toed down the hallway, glancing in the kitchen, but the noise came again from upstairs. And then it hit Noemie like lightning. She'd forgotten her shotgun. She vacillated at the bottom of the stairs, debating the wisdom of finding out who this intruder was.

The smart thing would be to turn around and skedaddle back to Montgomery's. But, of course, if she did that, she wouldn't know who was upstairs going through her belongings.

Noemie's heart beat like a terrified rabbit's and sweat popped out on her lip, but her anger was far more motivational. She picked up her skirt and inched up the stairs, purposely avoiding the ones that squeaked, and eased down the hallway to her bedroom.

He'd left the door ajar. She could see a man's shoulder

moving. He was sitting at her desk. Beside him, her strong box that she kept important items in was open. She slithered closer, silent as a cat, and peered through the cracked door.

Leroy was flipping through a stack of her papers as boldly as if he were at his own desk. He scanned each item quickly then moved on to the next.

What in the world...? Noemie couldn't imagine what he was looking for, but she was going to wring his neck for it. She was on the verge of barging in, but something held her back. She waited a second longer.

Leroy pulled a letter from its envelope, read the front, flipped it over, and paused. This letter he liked. A greasy grin lifted the corner of his lips as he folded it, tucked it back into its envelope, then dropped the letter in his pocket. He tapped the stack of papers into a neat pile and was about to drop them in the strong box when he noticed something. He reached in and came back with a twenty-dollar gold piece. Noemie's emergency fund.

Her blood boiled when he pocketed it, as well. She was done. Noemie flung the door open and yelled at the top of her lungs, "Leroy Heyward, you are a lowdown, lying thief!"

Leroy jumped to his feet, nearly knocking over the chair. "Noemie, what in tarnation are you doing here?"

"I live here," she bellowed at him, her fury blinding her to any sense. "You no-good, yellow-bellied piece of snakeskin."

"Now, Noemie," he raised his hands and began patting the air, "this ain't what it looks like. Calm down."

She stormed over to the desk. "You must be out of your ever-lovin' mind, coming into my house and stealing." She glared at him. "You oughtta be horse-whipped." She raised an accusing finger at him. "God help you if you had anything to do with Bear's death. I'll kill you myself."

Leroy licked his lips, ran a hand through pomade-slicked hair. "Noemie, I—I..." He held her gaze and she saw deep, icy fear seep into his eyes. Suddenly he sagged, his face drooped with sadness, and he dropped back into the chair. "I'm sorry." He wouldn't look at her. He shook his head, keeping his stare on the ground. "You're right, I am a lowdown scoundrel. I didn't have anything to do with what happened to Bear, but I'm here because I'm broke, Noemie." He brought his gaze back up to her. "And I'm about to lose everything."

———

MONTGOMERY WASN'T sure of everything he needed to say to Ruth, so he decided he'd start with what was, in his mind, the easiest. "I went into town this morning and took a look at the deed to Noemie's farm."

"And?"

"It's a fake. I'm sure of it."

"So Heyward's attempting to steal her farm? And that's why he didn't want us to see the deed?"

"I think so."

"How did ye figure the deed is a forgery?"

"I took Kenneth with me. I thought he might know what Noemie's signature looked like."

"And he did?"

"He brought with him a Christmas card Noemie sent a few years back."

"And the signatures didn't match?"

"Not even close."

"Well, then..."

"Yeah. Well then." He ran his hands up and down his suspenders. He wasn't sure what Noemie would do with this news. Nor could he figure out why Leroy had gone to the trouble to fake a deed if he were just going to give the woman her farm back.

"It's a crime," she said. "I suspect she'll want to prosecute him."

"You mean, if she doesn't shoot him."

Ruth laughed but it died quickly.

Montgomery would have to have some time to think through this Leroy mess. He knew he'd have to tell Noemie and just pray she didn't go off half-cocked. He dragged a hand over his mouth. Now it seemed like the time to address the other matter. He stopped walking and stared at the ground. "There's something else."

He pinched sweat off his upper lip, drummed his fingers on his thighs, exhaled a long breath. He felt like a foolish, witless teenager, and it annoyed him. He should trust his instincts. Whether they were right or wrong, though, what he wanted to say was going to change their relationship. Was he ready for it? He looked into her beautiful, delicate face and was taken aback by her bewildered expression, touched with desire. There he found his courage. "I'm forty-three, Ruth."

She blinked. "A good age. Seasoned but not too salty."

"My son is only four years younger than you."

"Oh, now..." Scowling, she tossed up a hand and took a step back. "I told ye, no more of that matchmaker business."

Montgomery grabbed her hand and she gasped. He savored the feel of her delicate fingers in his. Her skin was warm, her gaze shocked, but her countenance quickly gave way to smoldering desire. He swallowed his doubts. The air vibrated with heat and electricity. Their gazes, locked, were almost as physical as a touch.

He was old, but he wasn't dead. He pulled Ruth into his arms and pressed his lips to hers. The touch of her, the taste of her, rocked him. And when she relaxed and yielded to him, he nearly quit breathing. His hands marveled in the shape of her delicate waist, his whole being jolted at the feel of her curves pressed against him. His senses roared to life.

She moaned and he deepened the kiss. Light and heat mingled with the scent of earth and something uniquely, maddeningly her. So long since he'd held a woman, especially one that made him feel alive, all the way down to the deepest, loneliest corner of his heart.

He pulled away, amazed at the rollicking pace of his pulse and the rapid rise and fall of her breasts. He was light-headed. She smiled reassuringly and pulled him down to take her lips again. He felt for a moment as if he were holding on to the sun. He shook his head, tried to clear away this heady, mind-boggling fog she caused in him.

"I've never been very good with words, Ruth," he whispered apologetically, their noses touching. "My wife said I held too much back, expected her to just know things."

She tilted, caught his lips with hers. "Then let me say something."

He drifted his mouth over her cheek, across her forehead, and nodded.

"I feel safe when I'm with you, and like I'm on fire. And where I'm at right now feels like heaven. And home."

Montgomery grinned and nibbled at her lips. "The moment I saw you, something changed in my heart, Ruth. I tried to fight it. But when I thought Bear's death could have easily been you...the way I felt, I knew I was lost."

"Even then ye tried to pawn me off on another, younger man."

He tightened his grip on her, tilted her head so he could capture her attention. He hoped she could read the message in his eyes, but just in case, he'd make it plain. "I'm no young buck, Ruth, but I'm solid, steady...and in love with you."

She brushed strands of gray-streaked, caramel hair from his eyes. "No more matchmaking then?"

He clutched her fingers. "As a matter of fact, I've got the perfect man in mind...if you'll have him."

She stood on her tiptoes and slid her arms around his neck, a stretch for the petite little thing. "I believe I will."

CHAPTER NINETEEN

NOEMIE HAD ALWAYS PITIED LEROY. HE WAS LIKE A BAD-tempered, three-legged dog that everyone kicked out of the way. Mean had been a survival skill. He'd never fit in much as a kid, spent a lot of time alone, was mercilessly bullied. Everyone knew he had a daddy who beat him.

No better or kinder than the other kids, Noemie had joined in on the bullying, yet she'd seen the keen mind behind those beady eyes. Something told her, one day, he'd outgrow his awkward youth and find a path to success.

Apparently, he'd come close, but frittered away his opportunities. He sat at her desk now, a broken man, desperate enough to steal twenty dollars out of her strong box. Her pity took some of the steam out of her anger as she was not inclined to kick that three-legged dog when he was down. Oh, Leroy was going to jail. She felt he deserved it, but she reckoned she didn't have to be ugly about it. "Come on, let's go have some coffee and talk this out."

His eyes widened with surprise and relief and he nodded. "Yeah, I—I could use some coffee."

He followed her to the kitchen and sat down. She struck a match on the stove and lit the kindling. "So why did you steal the letter in your pocket?" He stiffened, then sighed. She opened up a canister of coffee and scooped some into the coffee pot. "What's going on, Leroy?" She paused at the sink. "You owe me an explanation," she said gently.

"You know, Noemie, I was doing pretty good there, for a while. I had picked up a few farms here and about. A couple of businesses. Had money rolling in. Started selling cotton down in Charleston." He fiddled with the placemat in front of him as she moved about making their coffee. "I was doing real well, but I couldn't ever seem to catch up with Montgomery."

Noemie sat down across from him to wait for the boil. "Why in tarnation did you care about competing with him?"

His brow creased. The wrinkles around his eyes deepened, his lips thinned. Years seemed to have come upon him in the matter of a few minutes. "I don't know. I just wanted to be the best at something for once in my life. But I got in over my head. I owe a lot of money. I needed a loan, so I used your farm as collateral."

"What? " she yelped, rising to her feet. Anger shot through her like a striking snake. "How did you manage that?"

"A fake deed," he said flatly.

"Are you saying there's a loan on this place?"

He shrugged a shoulder and looked at her with blank eyes. "The bank finds out I forged the deed, I reckon the loan won't stand. And they'll call it in...from me."

Noemie's mind whirled. What had he done? Would she be able to get out from under a note she didn't know anything about and was based on a forged document? Or was he really the one the bank would go after?

"You weren't supposed to be here, Noemie. Nobody ever comes back to Walhalla."

Fighting for control over the fury writhing in her veins, she sat back down. She was going to kill the man. Flat-out string him up if she found out her farm was in jeopardy. "Why'd you steal the letter? What's it say?"

"It's not the letter I was after. I needed to see your signature. I was going to clean up the deed, make sure the signatures matched, in case you took me to court."

Noemie clamped her jaw shut to keep from screaming at the man. The cold, selfish, thieving audacity of her cousin was almost more than she could bear. What crumb of pity she had for him disintegrated. She felt like leaping across the table and clawing out his eyes—but something in his gaze put the brakes on her fury. *Dead* was the word that came to her. Soulless. A lonesome, eerie feeling dragged its finger down her spine.

And then the meaning behind his words sa nk in. "You mean you were going to say I sold you the farm and, what, I was lying about the transaction, or forgot it al together?"

A cold, sharp edge gilded his expression. One eyebrow ticked up slightly. "Something like that." With astonishing speed, Leroy struck across the table and slapped Noemie so hard, she literally went down seeing stars...

———

MONTGOMERY HAD the inclination to hold Ruth's hand as they walked back to the wagon, but he tamped it down. "Ruth, you don't have to finish gleaning, I've got hired men I'd love to—"

"I'll finish today and let's talk to Noemie at supper. We'll figure things out."

The rattle of a wagon drew their attention. The reverend pulled up alongside Montgomery's conveyance, glanced at the group sitting in the shade, but then spotted Montgomery and Ruth. He tipped his hat at them and urged the horse forward.

"Afternoon. I was looking for Noemie. Thought I'd entice her to lunch."

"She's back at the house. Doing a little cleaning for me."

"Nah. She isn't. I stopped there first."

"Was she out back hanging laundry?" Ruth asked.

"I don't believe so. I looked."

Ruth and Montgomery exchanged glances. He knew they were thinking of Darla. And now another woman had vanished into thin air?

Ruth touched Montgomery's arm. "Most likely she went home. Don't ye think?"

Did he? The only thing he knew for sure was this twisting fear in his gut. Something was wrong. "Pastor, I'm gonna unhitch my horse and run over and check. You mind giving Ruth a ride back to the house and looking for Noemie again?"

"Of course not."

———

MONTGOMERY WAS GETTING a little old to be galloping over the mountain bareback, and he'd pay for it tomorrow, but an icy-hot fear skittered around and around in his gut. He guided the animal smoothly up the trail, skirting mountain laurel and tall pines. Noemie had no business going back to her farm alone, yet he knew that was exactly what she'd done.

God, protect that foolish, stubborn woman, please...

———

NOEMIE CAME-TO with a blinding pain behind her eyes and an uncomfortable, burning sensation in her scalp. Then she realized she was moving, being half-dragged, half-carried out the front door mostly by her hair, but there was an arm around her waist. Loose strands hung partially over her eyes, hindering her vision.

"Nobody ever comes back to Walhalla," Leroy grumbled.

Noemie blinked the fog from her brain, let her anger surge again. Remembering the slap across her face, she reached up and clawed him down the right cheek, growling like a wild cat as her nails dug into his flesh. He howled like a demon and dropped her. Instantly, she scrambled to her feet with the idea of lunging down the steps. She surged forward, but Leroy tackled her and they both rolled down the stairs, sharp jabs of pain exploding everywhere her bones connected with the edges.

On the ground, most of Leroy on top of her, Noemie threw a punch at his temple and then tried to claw him again. He grabbed her hands, and they wrestled for a moment. She was too livid to be afraid or wonder what he was planning. On a primal level, though, she knew she was fighting for her life. She jabbed a knee up into his groin hoping for a direct hit. Almost. Leroy blocked her, but not all the way. As he curled up reflexively, Noemie wriggled free.

She ran toward her horse, but Leroy lunged for her,

knocked her down again, cursing a blue streak. "Do not make me hurt you, cousin. Not yet."

As wild as a wolverine, Noemie howled, spittle flying from her mouth, as she screamed and fought the weight on top of her. Leroy raised his hand to slap her again. She blocked him by grabbing his wrist, but he used his other hand to wrap his fingers in her braid and snatched it hard to the side. Lightning bolts of pain shot up and down her neck.

"Confound you, woman, calm down."

God help you, Leroy, she thought, sinking her teeth into the side of his hand. He bellowed and raged, snatching his hand free. Blood gushed from the wound. "I'm gonna bury you next to Darla."

For an instant Noemie paused, but it felt like an eternity staring into black eyes full of malice and murder. The situation came home to her. Her fingers found a rock that fit nicely in her hand. "Not if I bury you first, Leroy." She drove the rock hard into his temple, but he lowered his head just enough at the last second to protect the vulnerable area.

The blow rattled him enough, however, that he loosened his grip on her. She had an instant to escape and clambered to her feet as he cradled his head and yowled in pain. She hiked up her skirt and ran for her horse, blind to anything but getting in that saddle.

Noemie was reaching out, almost there, when Leroy tackled her again. They rolled under the horse's feet. The mare scampered, stomped, and whinnied in fear. Noemie's head hit the ground so hard it bounced, and the pain reverberated through her skull like a drum. The light around her faded. She couldn't feel her body.

Yet, she could feel her arms rise over her head, feel the

gouge of a rock in the small of her back. She blinked and tried to clear her vision. Leroy towered over her, blood running from her claw marks and down from his scalp, fresh smears glistening on his hand. "Enough," he growled. Holding her wrists in a vice-like grip with one hand, he grabbed her bedraggled braid like a handle and began dragging her across the yard, toward the decimated kitchen garden. "I tried to warn ya, cousin. The hog. The stampede. Those deserters came in handy. I gave ya a chance, but you just wouldn't scare. And then you had to come back today. Just had to come back in the one hour I was here..."

"Stop, Leroy..." she whispered, clutching her braid to lessen the pain. Where was her voice? Darkness warred with the light in her eyes. *Can't let it win. Stay awake, Noemie.*

"Just like Darla. So high-and-mighty. Even when she moved back from Atlanta, still thought she was too good for me. Well, I showed her." He tugged on Noemie, as if for emphasis. "She should have been nice to me. You should have stayed in Maryland." He chuckled, but it was a winded, raspy sound. "And that boy in jail's gonna take my punishment." He whistled, a pleased sound. "It's all working out."

Noemie attempted to roll over and gain her feet but Leroy snatched her back, keeping her vulnerable as a turtle. She clawed at his hands. He shook her like a rag doll. "I was gonna write up a new deed with a lot better signature but now I don't reckon it matters."

Oh, Lord, Noemie prayed, her fury giving way to biting fear. *Help me. Help me, please.* She was weak, growing weaker with every step Leroy took. Her head thundered, her vision wasn't clear. The world was dim.

Growing dimmer.

"The bank won't be any...wiser." He was winded, breathing hard, gulping for breath. "That sounds like a plan, cousin." He stopped. "How can you be this heavy?" Still holding her braid, he leaned over, resting his hands on his knees. "This is too much work. I'll just kill you now."

He dropped her braid, stood up and scanned the garden. Alarm bells clanged in Noemie's head and she had a moment of jarring, brilliant clarity. She rolled away from him, grabbed a busted picket from the fence and before Leroy realized what was happening, she plunged it deep into his thigh. His howl of pain echoed off the mountains.

Run! A voice commanded Noemie. Once more, with the last bit of fading energy she had, she scrambled drunkenly to her feet. She was lifting her foot to run when Leroy spun her around. She saw his big fist coming down for a terrible blow—

The sound of a rifle shot thundered over them, reverberating in the air. Leroy's eyes widened. Blood exploded from his hand, spattering Noemie's face. He bellowed in pain and spun. Montgomery cocked the Springfield again and stared down the barrel. Leroy froze.

"Move away from her or the next one goes through your skull."

A DARKNESS ROSE UP in Montgomery that harkened back to bitter days. Alcohol had fed a beast in him long ago, before Maddie Sue, that liked the violence and destruction of feuding. His rifle barrel leveled on Leroy, he wanted to unleash the monster. Free him to pull the trigger and then dance on the man's grave. He prayed for Leroy to twitch an eyelid the wrong way.

Leroy lowered his bloody hand, pressed it to his chest, and covered it with his good hand. "You're gonna kill me, aren't you?"

The metal of the trigger warmed under Montgomery's finger. So easy to pull...

Noemie stumbled over to him and laid her hand gently on the barrel. "You ain't that boy no more, Montgomery," she rasped out, taking greedy breaths.

"He was gonna murder you." He kept his eyes on Leroy. "I suspect he's murdered Darla. You're responsible for Bear's death, too, aren't you?"

Leroy sucked on his teeth, taking his time to answer. "Not directly. It was unintended."

The evasive answer, empty of guilt or compassion, was like kerosene on Montgomery's mood. He just needed to strike the match. His finger tensed on the trigger—

"Montgomery," Noemie commanded in a hoarse voice. "Stop."

He blinked and eased off the trigger a little. The dark ocean between his soul and his brain receded a little. "What happened to Darla?"

Leroy's lip curled, but he didn't answer.

Montgomery teetered precariously between the man he was so long ago and the man Jesus had saved, made a better man. He speared Leroy with a look that was as cold and deadly as he could manage, but it hid his inner turmoil. He focused on the trigger beneath his finger, the power in it, the death in it. He could pu—

"All right, all right." Leroy raised his good hand. "She's buried on the mountain. Up near the spring."

Noemie winced.

Oh, Jesus, Montgomery thought. Grief propelled him forward. He crossed the space between him and Leroy so fast that the man only had time for one step back. Montgomery swung the butt of the rifle around like a club and clocked the man hard in the temple.

Leroy dropped like a dead bird.

———

RUTH STOPPED at the screen door and let out a soft, sad sigh. Noemie and Montgomery sat beside each other on the porch's top step, shoulders bent with grief, weariness, and heartache. The jingle of the sheriff's wagon was fading away in the settling dusk. Ruth rubbed her shoulders, still able to feel Leroy's murderous glare as Sheriff Holden secured him for the trip into town. To jail.

But the people she loved were safe from him.

Thank you, Jesus, they're both all right, she prayed again for the millionth time. *What would I do without them?*

"Would have never figured him capable of that," Noemie said, her voice husky with emotion. "I sure am glad you came along when you did."

Montgomery shook his head. "I knew you were here. And the closer I got, the more I knew you were in trouble."

After a long stretch of silence, Noemie sniffed. "God. He sent you to save me. He knew Leroy was gonna try to kill me."

"He sure looked intent on it."

"Makes me ashamed." Anger crept into her voice. "I'm just a hypocritical old fool."

"What?"

"One minute, I don't want anything to do with Him.

The next, just because somebody's trying to kill me, I call on Him for help."

"Well, I don't think that exactly surprised Him. Do you? You think He cares how or why the prodigal comes home?" Montgomery turned his head to look at her. "As long as she does?"

Kenneth stepped up behind Ruth, but she pressed a finger to her lips. Perhaps they shouldn't have been eavesdropping, but she felt the answer to her prayers was a breath away.

Noemie seemed to ponder the prodigal story, and then shrugged. "I reckon coming home *is* what matters."

"Bryl was thirteen when Maddie Sue passed away. He dealt with it poorly. He was angry at me, God, the world." Montgomery looked down at his hands. "One day, he decided to run away. Only, he ran into a crew of boys working on the Stumphouse tunnel. Hard cases. They took his money, his hat, and his shoes."

"Did they hurt him?"

"No, but it scared Bryl so bad he ran home, straight into my arms, crying like a baby." He chuckled. "Don't tell him I told you that part."

"I won't."

"Anyway, running away wasn't the smartest thing he'd ever done. Could have got himself killed. But that moment, when he was back in my arms safe and sound..." He took a deep breath. "That was all that mattered. You get my point?"

Noemie lowered her head. "I'm like Bryl. When people you love die, you want to lash out at something or someone. God's an easy target."

"Fathers usually are. Doesn't change how much they love you."

After a moment, Noemie shook Montgomery's knee playfully. "Thanks, boy. You and Ruth tried to tell me not to blame Him. He still loves me."

This seemed to end the conversation, and Ruth moved to push open the door when Montgomery spoke again and she stopped. "Noemie, I don't know if this is the time or not, but I want to talk to you about Ruth."

"Oh—" Ruth burst through the door, intent on stopping Montgomery. "Noemie, yer bath is ready, if ye are."

Montgomery shot her a suspicious look over his shoulder, but subtly ducked his chin in understanding.

Noemie slapped her thighs and rose stiffly to her feet. "You might have to come get me out in a little while so's I don't drown." She turned and paused at Kenneth's presence. "You still here?"

"I was hoping I might get an invite for supper."

"Well..." Noemie's cheeks actually reddened, to Ruth's delight. The woman brushed dirt off her skirt, but realized she was a mess all over and waved off the attempt. "You can take that up with Ruth. If she's of a mind to cook or not." She strode past them both, grabbed the screen door, and stopped. "Oh, I've got one question." She looked back at Montgomery. "When's the wedding?"

EPILOGUE

NOEMIE LAID HER HAND ON THE SCREEN DOOR BUT DIDN'T step outside. Montgomery held Ruth in a gentle embrace as the couple gazed out over the hills alive now with jubilant fall colors. In the moment, they were living and loving and she couldn't interrupt.

Their union made her smile. And then a shadow swept over her heart. James wouldn't be the one to bring about her grandchildren. His memory, the life he lived here on this earth, would fade away to nothing but a weedy tombstone. No legacy to pass on. Same for Bear, too. Lives that had barely gotten started, snuffed out.

She raised her chin and swallowed. She loved Ruth like a daughter, though, and would have killed to see her happy. Montgomery was a good man. He'd love her and honor her till death parted them. Maybe even beyond. Who knew?

A hand slipped around Noemie's waist and Kenneth whispered in her ear, "The turkey is ready to carve."

She clutched his hand and smiled, bashful about the goosebumps the *pastor* raised on her skin. His warm breath on her ear and neck gave her chills. *How, Lord, have I managed to fall in love again?* She bit her lip. *With him and You. Thank You.*

"I've had a scripture going round and round in my head," he whispered, his breath still tickling her ear. "Now the Lord blessed the latter days of Job more than his beginning."

Noemie was surprised by the tightening in her throat and fought it back before she spoke again. "I'm almost as happy as Ruth out there." She squeezed his hand. "God is good, isn't He, Kenneth?"

He kissed her head tenderly. "Yes, He is, Noemie. He surely is."

FALL IN OCONEE COUNTY took Ruth's breath away. The riot of colors on the hills and mountains stopped her in her tracks as she strolled down the porch. Leaves of burnt sienna, vibrant scarlet, and deep gold danced on the trees, the colors joyously painting the surrounding landscape. The air, too, was simply magnificent. Warm, but not hot, dry without being harsh. It made her feel light and airy, like a feather. The cloudless cornflower blue sky overhead begged her to soar into its vastness. The beauty of it and the blessings around her nearly took her breath away.

"You look starstruck."

She grinned over her shoulder at Montgomery. He slipped up behind her, folding her into an embrace, and rested his chin on her head. She nestled against him, almost moved to tears with joy. For a moment, she couldn't speak.

"Aren't you talking to me?"

"Ye'll think me silly."

"Try me."

"I am so blessed it makes me want to cry."

He chuckled softly, comfortingly. "There is nothing silly about that."

She twirled in his arms, lifted her face to him, and laid her hands on his suspenders. "Are ye sure you want to live here? Ye've a beautiful home that ye built—"

"For another woman, another life." He stroked her cheek with the back of his hand, his eyes, blue as the sky above, sparkled with happiness and peace. "You and Noemie are two of my favorite people in the world. I couldn't be happier here." He kissed her, and his touch turned her insides to jelly, made her heart leap in her chest. She reveled in his soft lips nibbling hers. And even when he wasn't touching her, she felt loved, cared for, watched over. How she adored this man.

"Besides," he added, kissing her nose, "If I'm here, Bryl can bring that new bride of his to the old home place."

"Strange, isn't it? Father and son marrying in the same month."

"I'd call it fortunate." He shook his head, as if astonished by something. "In one fell swoop, I've gained a wife, a mother-in-law, a daughter-in-law, and soon, I'd bet, grandbabies."

Ruth sucked in a breath. She hadn't thought of that. She might be a grandmother before she was a mother.

Montgomery wiggled his eyebrows at her, giving her a come-hither look that made the jelly inside her quiver. "Maybe we could beat them to the punch," he suggested seductively. "I'm not too old to raise a passel of my own children." He kissed her again, with a little more heat this time, as if to prove it, and Ruth felt the blood rush from her head to her feet.

Noemie cleared her throat to announce her presence and pushed the screen door open a few inches. Ruth and Montgomery grudgingly parted.

"Turkey's on the table, you two. Come on in...and let's give thanks."

A LOOK AT: A GOOD MAN COMES AROUND

A heart-stirring tale of brokenness, redemption, and the faith that binds hearts back together.

Oliver Martin is done—with hope, with God, and most especially with women. When his well-meaning friend sends for a wife on his behalf, Oliver makes it clear he's not husband material. Abigail Holt agrees. The last thing she wants is another bitter, drunk, and spiritually lost man anywhere near her or her young sons.

But when a tragic loss leaves Oliver staring down the mess he's made of his life, a single, soul-deep question arises: Can a man who's fallen so far ever rise again?

As grief turns to grace and harsh judgments shift to healing, Abigail begins to see what her heart never dared to hope for: a good man worth loving—if she can only trust again.

Based on a true story of a gold strike that changed everything, this Western Romance offers a powerful tale of second chances, stirring faith, and the kind of love that doesn't just heal—but transforms.

Can a broken man become the blessing he was meant to be? And can a guarded heart learn to love again—without losing everything?

AVAILABLE DECEMBER 2025

ABOUT THE AUTHOR

Heather Blanton is a *USA Today* bestselling author of thirty Christian Western romances, including the highly rated and awarded Romance in the Rockies series. She is also an award-winning script writer. Her Romance in the Rockies series has been optioned for a limited TV series, and her script *Unbridled Hearts* is currently optioned as well.

She grew up in the mountains of Western North Carolina on a steady diet of *Bonanza, Gunsmoke,* and John Wayne Westerns. Her daddy taught her to shoot when she was five, and she can hit that at which she aims.

Her novels are all Christian Western romance because she enjoys creating feisty pioneer women who struggle to find love and hold on to their faith. Like all good, old-fashioned Westerns, there is always justice, a moral message, American values, lots of high adventure, unexpected plot twists, and often a touch of suspense.

www.authorheatherblanton.com